THE MARRIAGE BARGAIN

Tales From The Brazos

NANCY SMITH GIBSON

SOUL MATE PUBLISHING

New York

THE MARRIAGE BARGAIN

Copyright©2016

NANCY SMITH GIBSON

Cover Design by Melody A. Pond

This book is a work of fiction. The names, characters, places, and incidents are the products of the author's imagination or are used fictitiously. Any resemblance to actual events, business establishments, locales, or persons, living or dead, is entirely coincidental.

Published in the United States of America by
Soul Mate Publishing
P.O. Box 24
Macedon, New York, 14502

ISBN: 978-1-68291-353-6

ebook ISBN: 978-1-68291-078-8

www.SoulMatePublishing.com

The publisher does not have any control over and does not assume any responsibility for author or third-party websites or their content.

Dedicated to my children

Lisa, Robin, Holly, and Joel

Thank you for encouraging me in this,

The latest of my endeavors

Your support means

The world to me.

Acknowledgements

My deepest thanks to all those who helped me get this book written and published. My special thanks to the Hot Springs Critique and Feedback Group, who listened and made suggestions to improve the story. Special thanks are due to my diligent editor, Tamus Bairen, without whom this novel would be full of mistakes.

Chapter 1

The hawk circled high above. His sharp eye was on the ground; nothing escaped his attention. He was waiting on his next victim—any small creature that ventured out of hiding and into his keen site. He missed nothing.

The field mouse crouched in a tall clump of grass and watched. There was a bit of sustenance there, just beyond its reach. Finally, it darted out to grab a bite of dinner. As quick as a sparkle of light, the hawk dove, but the mouse had seen the shadow foretelling the enemy's arrival and scurried down a rabbit hole.

The hawk resumed circling. He kept his eyes on that rabbit hole. The mouse had to come out sometime . . . and he'd be waiting.

"Man! It's sure heatin' up. I'll be glad when we get all this fence run." The short, wiry worker bent his head sideways and wiped the sweat from his face with his shoulder.

"Running fence is a never-ending job. Soon as you check it all, some wayward momma cow or angry bull takes it down again, and it's all to do over." The tall, tanned cowboy pulled a bandana from the pocket of his Levis and wiped his face.

"Yeah, well, at least it's a job, I guess." The sinewy older man put his wire pliers into his saddlebag and unhooked his canteen from the saddle horn.

"Better than not having one, I reckon." The younger man tucked his pliers into his back pocket and reached for his water, relishing the thought of a cool mouthful.

They both looked up as the sounds of hoof beats signaled that someone was coming.

"Hey, Kelso! You come to help us?" the old man asked.

"Nah, Gaines, you're the expert on fixin' fence wire. Crandall, Boss wants to see you up at the Big House, pronto!"

"Whatcha gone and done, Crandall, to get in trouble with the Boss?"

"No idea," he said with a surety he didn't feel inside. He took another swallow of water. "Any idea what it's about?" he asked Kelso.

"I don't know beans about it. Boss just said fetch you, so I did." He wheeled his horse. "I gotta get back to doin' my own chores." He took off at a lope.

"I reckon I might as well get on back to the spread, too," Gaines said. "This is pretty much a two-person job."

"We can finish it tomorrow," Crandall said as he swung up onto his horse.

Dorie wrung the water out of the washrag and applied the cool cloth to her face. It provided a brief respite from the heat and nausea that had been plaguing her. Folding the square of fabric over the towel rack, she used a brush to tame her hair, straightened the collar of her housedress, and with one final glance in the mirror, left the bathroom.

It was a bit cooler on the lower floor. The porch that sheltered the front and half of each side of the big farmhouse shaded the rooms, and Annie kept the shades pulled almost to the bottom of each window. The huge oak trees provided shade on all sides, giving the impression of serene greenness. When Dorie entered the kitchen, she found the housekeeper with her head in the refrigerator.

"Are you looking for something, Annie, or are you just trying to stay cool?" Dorie joked.

"Huh. Not doin' any good. What you gonna want for dinner?"

"Not much. This heat has killed my appetite. Do we have any tea made?"

"Yes, ma'am, we do." She pulled a pitcher from the top shelf. "I'll get you some ice. That ought to cool you off some." She took a tray from the small freezer section and carried it to the sink. Pulling up on the metal lever, some cubes popped loose. She put a few into a glass, poured the amber liquid, and handed it to Dorie. "I think I'll fix me a glass, too." She repeated her actions and took a long swallow. "This ought to cool us both off."

"I'm going to be in the office, Annie. I've called over to the barn and asked Burt to send Crandall to see me. When he comes, show him where to go, please."

"Yessum, I will. That sure is one fine-looking man. Wish he was a tad older and had a bit of Indian in him. I'd be looking at him a mite harder."

Walking down the hall toward the office, the younger woman thought, *I wish he wasn't so good looking. It makes what I'm going to do that much harder.*

Chapter 2

He held his hat in his hand as the Indian woman took him down the hall. A shiver ran down his spine and goosebumps formed on his arms as he contemplated what it would do to his plans if he lost this job. He liked it on the Big B Ranch, and he was right where he needed to be. Everything was working out . . . well, almost everything.

The door stood open, and the maid said, "Gentleman to see you, Miss Dorie."

"Come in, please." She was sitting behind a mahogany desk that was so large it made her look even smaller than she was. "Close the door, Annie, please." She wasn't smiling, and he thought that must be a bad sign.

"Have a seat." She indicated a wingback chair across the desk from her. A glass sat at her elbow. It was empty, and he wondered if she stayed as thirsty as he did during this heat. He had thought her pretty when he saw her around the ranch, and now her skin had a moist glow to it, and her hair formed ringlets around her face. He wondered if she would taste salty if he put his tongue to the side of her neck. His thoughts were interrupted when she addressed him.

"Mr. Crandall." She stopped and looked at her hands, which were wrapped together in front of her. "Mr. Crandall . . ."

Uh-oh. Here it comes. She's going to fire me. But why? And why is she so nervous about it? Everyone says she's a tough boss. She's bound to have fired people before.

"I have to ask you to promise me something." She looked up, staring at him intently, as if trying to judge something about him. "I have to ask that what I am about to discuss you will keep to yourself. You must not repeat any of this to anyone, anywhere."

"All right." *What's going on here?*

"I need your word as a gentleman. You are a gentleman, aren't you?"

His anger almost rose at that, but he held steady. "Yes. I'm a gentleman, and I'll keep your secret." She remained silent, and he added, "On my word as a gentleman."

Evidently she was waiting on that assurance. She took a deep breath and spoke. "I'm going to offer you a business proposition. Please hear it through entirely and take some time before you answer me. Not too much time. Say, twenty-four hours."

He sat back in his chair. Business propositions he understood. Why this one had to be a secret, he didn't know, yet he would before long, and he'd think long and hard about it. He wasn't about to get snookered by some shady deal. *The boss doesn't have a reputation for being devious in her transactions, but you can't be too careful. At least it doesn't sound as if I'm being fired.*

She didn't look like a dishonest person, either. She wasn't a young girl anymore. She'd probably passed her thirtieth birthday, but she was slim and nice looking. Her skin was smooth and unblemished and lightly tanned from being out in the sun as she kept up with her ranch. Her blond hair had light streaks scattered throughout, and her hazel eyes were clear and bright. She wasn't a flapper—far from it. Her skirts came below her knees, and there was no flirty attitude about her. No giggles. No sidelong glances. All business, her demeanor was in no way suggestive of anything except exactly what she was saying. When she came to the barn, she talked with the foreman, Burt, and went back to the Big House, never giving a side-glance to the men who happened to be around.

Her long fingers played with a scrap of paper she kept nervously folding and unfolding. Finally, she dropped it. "I find that, for business reasons, I am in need of a husband. It is not necessary for you to know why."

His eyes widened involuntarily. This was not what had been flickering through his thought processes. *Is she proposing to me?*

"It would be in name only, you understand. You would live here, in this house, with me. We would not share a bedroom." A blush stained her cheeks. "But that part would be a secret to the world. As far as anyone else is concerned, it would be a normal marriage. It is important that everyone believes that it is."

She didn't look at him now. He wouldn't have thought she could become embarrassed. To someone raised on a ranch, the matter of having separate bedrooms shouldn't cause the red that appeared on her cheeks. *Is it possible she's still a virgin? Yeah, I bet she is. Just the thought of what a man and woman do in bed discomfits her.*

"The marriage wouldn't last forever, just . . . maybe a year."

"A year?"

"Yes. After a year, we would divorce."

They both sat in silence, thinking about their own part in such a situation. After a minute, she said, "You would be recompensed for your time, of course."

"Recompensed?"

"Yes. It means . . ."

"I know what it means." *So she doesn't think I'm very bright. Maybe she thinks she can get something by me.*

"I just meant it wouldn't be right for you to do something for me for nothing. I thought . . ." She picked up the scrap of folded paper and started refolding it again. "I thought double your present salary ought to be fair."

She sat back in the oversized office chair. "I would provide you with a wardrobe suitable for your position as my husband and an automobile so you could get around. All of it would be yours when we divorce."

So she wants me to be her . . . what? Not a paramour. Not a gigolo, not that. Nothing more than a paid . . . husband who isn't really a husband. It's not taking money for sex. So what's the problem? It means security . . . security right now when I need it most. But . . .

"Haven't you forgotten something?

Her eyes opened wider. "Oh! Yes! I should have asked right off. Are you married?"

"No, I'm not married."

"Do you have sweetheart? A fiancée?"

"No. None of that. What I was referring to was my job and how I would fit into the organization and running of your ranch. I don't see that I could continue working with the men the way I have been."

Her eyes narrowed. "There would be no change in the running of my ranch. It would still be *my* ranch. Burt would continue to be foreman. You would have no say-so in the operation. You would get no part of it when we divorce."

"I didn't expect I would, but do you expect me to work alongside the men like I do now? It just might be a bit testy for the boss's husband to be right there with them, listening to everything they say, maybe reporting back."

Dorie was quick with decisions. She had to be, running a complex operation as she did. "I'd give you free rein to find what job you wanted to do on the ranch, but you couldn't interfere with anything Burt says or does . . . or me either. And you couldn't boss the men. That's Burt's job."

That might be a problem. There might be a lot of hurt feelings, even jealousy on Burt's part. He's a good man, but still, the idea of the boss's husband hanging around, not taking orders. Well, maybe I could work through that.

The window behind her was open, and a breeze lifted strands of her hair. *A storm must be brewing. We could use*

the rain, and I hope it comes, but Sarah is afraid of thunder.
I hope . . .

"One more thing." He looked back at her. Her cheeks were flushed once again. "I know that men have certain . . . needs. I will not be shamed in this community. If you find that you need female companionship, you must seek it far enough away from Cottonport, or even this county, that no one will ever know. Maybe you could go to Houston, or Dallas."

"Using my new auto that you are going to buy me?" The sarcasm escaped her.

Chapter 3

Crandall left the porch in one bound and strode to where his dusty Ford pickup sat. He tried to still his thoughts, but everything that popped into his head seemed to lead back to the unusual offer he had just been presented. The truck was a '23 model, only ten years old, but it had been through a lot. He wouldn't take a car as a gift from this woman—or any woman—but if he went along with the outlandish deal she had offered, he would have enough money to fix up his vehicle, at least to the point he could make sure it would start whenever he wanted it to, without getting money from home, alerting anyone there about where he was and what he was up to.

It only took a few tries before it cranked right up, and he prodded it down the road. It was late afternoon, and he had no sense of need to get back to work. *What will she do if I lay off the rest of the day? Fire me?* He snorted at the thought.

Down the road a few miles, it was obvious that a rain had moved through not long before. The dust had settled, and the smell of wet fields was as glorious as any perfume could be. He breathed deeply. *Better store up the memory. Not much telling how long it'll be before we get another rain.*

A half-hour later, he pulled up in front of a small, white frame house on the outskirts of a town a few miles from Cottonport. As soon as he got out of the truck, he saw the small, forlorn figure on the front porch. A shy smile greeted him as he climbed the steps.

"Hi there, Punkin!"

"Hi."

At least she's speaking. That's better than usual. He got

down on one knee in front of her. "Are you OK? What have you been doing since last time I was here?"

The child shrugged her shoulders, her eyes on the fold of her faded dress she was twisting.

"It looks like it's been raining here. Did it thunder?"

The girl looked at him then back at her fingers. She nodded. "It scared me." He started to ask if Mrs. Finch had held her and comforted her when she was frightened, but he knew the answer to that question, and asking it would only reinforce to the child that she was alone with no one to turn to.

A woman came to the screen door and pushed it open.

"There you are, Mr. Crandall. We was wonderin' if you had forgotten all about us. That's the way of men, to put women away and forget about 'em." He could have attacked the woman, if only verbally, for the suggestion that he would ever forget Sarah.

"Never, Mrs. Finch. I would never forget my niece." He stood to his full height, reached down, and swung the girl into his arms. He held her tight and tried to communicate his love through his touch.

"I have your money for you," he said and reached into his shirt pocket, pulling out bills. "Five dollars for the month. Paid in full." The woman counted the bills carefully then folded them and stuck them into the front of her dress. "She looks thin. Be sure she's getting plenty to eat. I want her fed well."

"Oh, she's fed plenty. She just don't eat. She's picky."

He looked at the child resting on his shoulder, her tiny arms around his neck. "Then feed her something she likes!"

"Humph." The woman looked away. "Well, see here, this is the last month I'll be able to keep her, anyway. My husband is coming home from . . . well, he's coming home, and he don't like for nobody else to be in the house when he's here. You come get her before the end of the month. Hear?" She turned and went back into the house, the screen door slamming behind her.

Chapter 4

The next morning Crandall rose even earlier than usual. Taking soap and a towel, he made his way to the outdoor shower that was rigged up on the side of the bunkhouse. Bathed and freshly shaved, he dressed in clean britches and a laundered shirt. He was one of the first people at the cook shack, where he only had stomach for a biscuit and cup of coffee.

"What's the matter, Crandall?" Cookie asked. "My cookin' don't suit you no more?"

"Your victuals are just fine. It's just this heat. It kills my appetite."

"You got that right! Women and one hundred degree temperatures . . . they can sure play hell with a man's hungriness, all right." Cookie wandered away to give some other man lip.

He doesn't know how right he has it, Crandall thought.

It was much too early to present himself at the Big House. Everyone at a ranch rose early, especially in the summer when it was daylight by five and you wanted to beat the heat, but he didn't think the boss would appreciate him showing up so early. He went to his truck and sat in it, wondering if he was letting himself in for more worry instead of relieving his problems. At this point, he didn't have many choices, and this one seemed to be the best, or at least the easiest.

When he saw Burt's truck pull up to the barn, where the foreman's office was located, he got out and walked over, his boots making small clouds of dust along the way.

"Morning, Crandall. You're up and ready mighty early. You and Gaines gonna get back on that fence this mornin'?"

"I came by to tell you I have to go do something for the boss this morning. I don't know if I'll get back to the fence or not."

"That's two days in a row," the foreman said. With a twinkle in his eye, he asked, "You and the boss got somethin' goin' on I ought to know about?"

He had thought about this—how to deflect questions and jokes. The best way was with another joking comment. The fellows were always putting each other on. They would take it as just that, until the news leaked out, of course. Not much tellin' how it'd be after that.

"Yeah, that's it. You figured us out." He walked toward the open door where he had entered. "But don't tell anybody. We're keeping it a secret."

Burt snickered. "Well, let me know when she's through with you, and I'll put you to work again." He started toward the door to his office. "If you have any energy left, that is!" He broke into a guffaw.

When he knocked on the big mahogany front door with the beveled glass insert, the same Indian woman opened it. "Yes?" She frowned. Obviously his arrival was unexpected.

"I'd like to speak with Miss Barnett, please."

"I'll see." She closed the door but didn't push it until it latched. Not a complete rejection. It missed that by about an inch.

Minutes passed before she returned. Swinging the door open, she stood aside and said, "She'll be down in a little bit. You can wait for her in the office." It was obvious from her tone of voice and demeanor that she could just as well have been telling him to go to hell as to have been welcoming him into the house. She let him precede her down the hall. *Probably watching to be sure I don't steal anything.* When he entered the office, he took a seat in the same wingback chair he had sat in the previous day and gave her a big smile. She said nothing but shook her head and left, mumbling something in what he took to be the language of her ancestors.

It was a comfortable, welcoming room, especially if you were a reader. One wall was all shelves, and they were very nearly filled with books. Almost, but not quite. A few framed photographs were stuck in here and there, not in positions of importance, but as if they were afterthoughts—required accoutrements of the room but not images that demanded attention. The desk had stacks of papers on it, waiting for the attention of the person in charge of the county's biggest cattle operation. In the far corner was an overstuffed chair, the perfect place to settle in with an interesting book on a rainy afternoon when ailing cattle, stock prices, or other ranch matters didn't keep you from fantasizing about foreign lands or exotic adventures.

A faded oriental rug covered the center of the area, muffling footsteps that might intrude on the feeling of solitude the place conveyed. The only sound that whispered through the room was the soft ticking of a clock, marking the passage of time in a room that looked as if time stood still.

"I'm sorry to keep you waiting." She came in a rush, bringing the scent of soap with her, the ends of her hair still wet. "I didn't expect you back so soon."

"You said you needed an answer within twenty-four hours."

"Yes. Yes, I did." *She looks worried. Maybe she thinks taking only fifteen of the twenty-four means I'm going to reject the proposal.* "And you have decided?"

"I have a couple more questions first."

"Yes. Of course. Whatever you need to know."

"You said I could decide on whatever work I would do. Is it all right with you if there are times I am not busy at ranch work?"

She looked puzzled. "You mean not work? Or work at something that is not ranch related?"

"Yes."

"Yes. That would all right with me." She went to the chair behind the desk and sat down. "But I couldn't put up with it if . . ."

"If what?"

"If you lay about drinking." She said it quickly and quietly.

"In other words, you won't put up with a drunk."

She straightened her shoulders and stuck her chin out. Her tone of voice conveyed her determination, and he imagined she would tell him the deal was off if he got drunk every night. "That's right."

"That's fine. I'm not much of a drinker." She visibly relaxed.

"I have one more term. Without this, I have to refuse."

She looked at him quizzically. "And it is?"

"I have a child who is my responsibility . . ."

"Oh! You have a child!"

"Not exactly. She isn't my child, but I am responsible for her." He wanted to explain, make it clear how important Sarah was in his life, but he didn't want to go into too much detail. He had secrets, too—secrets that were best not laid bare for the world to be privy to. "I want to bring her to live here, too. I *need* to bring her here. And having her here, I may need to tend to her instead of work on the ranch."

"I . . . I see." She didn't, of course.

"If I can't bring her, if I can't see to her, I can't do it . . . marry you, that is. Live here in this house."

"Oh."

"In fact, if I can't do it this way, I may have to quit altogether, so I can see to her."

He hadn't really understood, until he said it aloud, how true that was. Nothing was more important than Sarah's well-being. The harpy he had used for temporary care was a mistake. He saw that now. If the boss didn't accept his terms, then he'd have to leave, and his plan would fail before it ever began.

"I don't see why that wouldn't work," she said. "This is a big house. There are plenty of bedrooms. And since it would be problematic for you to work as one of the men after we are married—if we are married"—she quickly corrected herself—"you could spend as much time as necessary tending to your . . . her."

He took a deep breath. "Then I accept your business proposal." *Please, God, let me be doing the right thing.* His mother always told him to have faith. He thought he would have to have a lot to enter into this crazy arrangement and think it would be the best for everyone involved, especially Sarah.

"Fine! Good!" She stood and walked around the desk. "I'll start making plans. This needs to happen in the next day or so!"

That quickly! This business, whatever it is, sure must be important, to have to have a husband in such a hurry. She'll have to pull together a wedding . . . I hope it's not too fancy.

"Let me make some phone calls, find out some things. Why don't you come back this afternoon? By then I'll know what we ought to do next."

"That sounds good to me. Gaines and I need to finish running the fence we were working on." He walked to the office door. His hand was on the knob when she stopped him.

"Mr. Crandall, I guess if we're going to be married I need to know your first name."

"It's Jonah."

"Jonah, my first name is Isadora, but my family called me Dorie."

"I'll see you after lunch, Boss . . . er . . . Dorie."

Chapter 5

Dawn was breaking the next morning when Jonah arrived at the Big House. Dorie's car had been brought up from the barn where it was kept, and he parked his old truck beside it.

Evidently she had been watching for him because, as soon as he arrived, the front door opened and she came out onto the porch. She spoke quietly, conscious of how voices carry in still night air. "I have my suitcase, if you'll load it for me."

He gained the porch in one bound and entered the dark hallway as she held the door open for him.

"It's at the top of the stairs." Dorie pointed in the direction of the staircase.

The oriental runner muffled his footsteps as he quickly went up, grabbed the handle of the leather valise, and returned to the foyer. She gathered her handbag and gloves from the side table, gave herself a cursory glance in the mirror, and went out the door. He closed it behind himself.

Her automobile was the latest in style. He thought it was unexpected for a woman who was all business to be driving an Auburn Speedster. He had only seen her in the old pickup she drove around the ranch, never in this expensive car. "Nice car," he said as he deposited her suitcase in it.

"It was my birthday present to myself. They were on sale. Trying to boost the economy, you know."

He did know about the economy. Knew that it was bad, very bad, and people were suffering all over the country, although there were no signs of it on the ranch.

"I'll get my bag." Jonah went to his truck and retrieved a well-worn piece of luggage containing the few clean clothes he had. He tossed it in with hers. *The beginning of a marriage. Two suitcases going on a trip together. Two strangers going along.*

"Should I move my truck to some place it won't be obvious?"

"Annie is going to have someone come move it." She was wrapping a scarf around her head.

"Annie? Is that the Indian woman who works for you?"

"Yes." She opened the driver's door and slid behind the wheel. "Get in."

She was still the boss. He obeyed her order. The car roared to life, and by the time they reached the road, she had hit top gear. She never slowed up as she pulled out onto the highway.

"There is something you ought to know. Something I am particular about," Dorie said. She had to speak loudly to be heard over the rushing wind.

"Yes?"

"You may call her Mrs. Runningdeer, or if she permits, you may call her Annie, but under no circumstances are you ever to call her squaw, or Pocahontas, or any other derogatory term."

He raised his eyebrows. *What brought that about?* "I wouldn't think of it."

"Good."

With that, she increased the speed. Soon, they were flying over the roadway. She seemed at ease, as if she drove like a demon every day. After a while, he gathered his nerve to speak. "The speed limit is 45 miles per hour anywhere in the state."

"I want to get to Houston by late morning."

He said no more.

"We'll take the three suits, those trousers, and the other ones on the table. He'll need a dozen or so shirts. And smallclothes, of course."

The pile was growing. When she directed Jonah to the menswear shop, he had no idea what he was in for. He tried to argue, but Dorie shushed him. "You have to fit into my life, remember." Fitting in meant dressing properly, he guessed. There was no way to argue without making a scene, and he didn't want to embarrass her or himself in that way.

"We are going to get a bite of lunch. When we return, we need that pair of trousers"—she pointed to a pair of light gray pants Jonah was wearing—"altered as to length. We will return the day after tomorrow. You will have the rest of the trousers altered by then, will you not?"

The clerk stammered and stuttered, but finally agreed. "If the gentleman will try on each pair for the in-house tailor to measure, madam's wishes will be met."

"I thought you could do it."

When Jonah returned from the dressing room, where he put his original clothes back on, she took his arm. "Let's go to that little coffee shop down the block and have lunch. I didn't feel like eating breakfast, and I'm hungry."

Less than an hour later, they were back at the shop. Jonah's gray trousers were ready. When they left, the purchases were so many that a salesclerk had to assist them in getting the packages to the car. "Wow!" The young man ran his eyes over the Auburn. "This is some car you have, sir!"

"It's hers," Jonah said, nodding his head toward Dorie. *If I didn't already feel like I was going to be a kept man, I sure do now!*

Dorie acknowledged the compliment with a small smile. "Thank you." She extended her gloved hand and handed the young man some coins.

"Where to now?" Jonah asked when he climbed in the Auburn.

"Galveston," came the answer as she started the engine. "Why Galveston?"

She pulled out from the curb, driving at a slightly slower speed since they were in a busy metropolis. "You can get things done in Galveston that you can't anywhere else. We can get married without going through all the rules and regulations we would have anyplace else. All it takes is money. And it will be almost impossible to track what we've done and when." With that, their speed increased, and they were off again.

Sometime later, they approached the long causeway leading from the mainland to the island. Jonah considered himself a fairly brave man. He had been in some harrowing situations in his life and had handled himself well, but this was different, *I'm sure glad I can swim. Oh, don't be lily-livered, man. Thousands of cars drive over this every day. At least she's slowed down . . . a little.*

"This doesn't make you nervous?" he asked as a train roared by right next to them.

"This? No. Once you get used to it, it's OK."

He looked down at the water on the other side. "Wonder how deep the water is here?"

"Oh, don't be a wuss. We're a long way above the water." He looked at her, eyebrows raised. She looked back. "Seventeen feet—the water is seventeen feet down from us. I don't know how deep it is. Pretty deep, I'd guess, but they say the pilings that hold this up go sixteen feet down into the ground below the water."

"Keep your eyes on the road, please."

"Oh, for goodness sake!" She returned her mind and eyes to the road. After a minute she said, "This causeway is a lifesaver for Galveston Island. It's been worth every penny of the three million it cost to build it."

Jonah was becoming slightly more accustomed to skimming what he thought of as the tops of the waves and could think of something other than what he would do if they suddenly plunged over the side into the water. "I would imagine so. It makes it easier to get people and merchandise back and forth."

"Yes. They were in bad shape after the big hurricane hit. Galveston could have never recovered the way they have without being able to move people and product back and forth the way they do." An electric railcar glided by, headed toward Houston. "The Interurban Train helps people to get to work on the other side, whichever way they want to go, and now there is a way to get enormous amounts of people off the island in case of another hurricane. People won't perish like they did in 1900."

"I can see that the causeway helps, but what about the ships that need to go through here? Doesn't this block them?"

"There is a lift gate to let them through. I hope we don't get caught by it. We'd be sitting here as long as it takes the ship to pass."

Soon enough they reached the other side. He was looking forward to seeing the famed city. When Dorie had told him where they were going, he was surprised at first. Galveston was known as Sin City. It was said that anything and everything went on there: gambling, illegal liquor, prostitution. It didn't seem like the kind of place she would frequent. Then it made sense to him. They could probably circumvent any laws that would prevent them from marrying immediately—laws that would cause a problem anywhere on the mainland.

"Here we are! Galveston!" Dorie said as they reached the buildings that signaled they had gained Galveston City. They passed cafes, souvenir shops, houses painted in all sorts of bright colors—pink, yellow, blue, green—and palm trees. Jonah had seen palm trees the times he had been to Houston, but never in such abundance. It was like they were in another world.

He didn't know what he had been expecting, but it wasn't a bustling city. It looked clean and well-kept. *I guess I thought sin would be messier than this. Seedy, maybe, or unkempt. This looks prosperous.*

It was obvious when they reached the business district. The buildings were taller and decorated in more of a traditional style, with stonework imitating that of their cousins on the mainland. Dorie turned one way, then another, and finally pulled into a parking spot in front of the Galveston County Courthouse.

"We need to get a marriage license," she said.

"Oh. I forgot something," Jonah muttered.

"What did you forget?"

"A ring. We need a ring. Is there a place where I can buy one?"

"No need. I have one."

For the first time, Jonah felt a twinge of something—guilt or embarrassment maybe. "A woman shouldn't have to provide her own wedding ring. Not in any circumstance," he told his bride-to-be.

"It was my mother's. I would have wanted to use it in any circumstance." She reached into her purse and took out a small box. "I just hadn't thought it would be used in this way." She handed it to him and reached into the bag again. "I'm going to give you some money. The man usually pays for things. If we don't want to stand out, you need to be the one paying."

His heart fluttered at the size of the roll of bills she handed him. "OK, but you may have to give me some pointers along the way." Nothing he had ever done in his life had prepared him for what was happening at that moment.

She smiled. "I will, but you'll do fine. We'll go in here and get the license. If there is any hang-up, slide a bill casually toward the clerk and say, 'Is there any way we can get around this problem?'"

He stared at her, eyebrows raised.

"I learned that from my father."

Twenty minutes later, they had their license, and he hadn't had to bribe anyone. It wasn't that he was against bribes, but it seemed auspicious that the marriage was starting without resorting to minor lawbreaking at the very beginning. The next hurdle, however, was pointed out when the clerk said, "That license won't be valid for seventy-two hours. We have a waiting period, you know." Dorie smiled and said, "Yes. Thank you."

When they got back in the car, Jonah asked, "So, are we going to wait three days to get married?"

"Of course not."

"I didn't think so."

She eased the car away from the curb, driving more sedately in town. They wove their way through downtown to Seawall Boulevard and headed south along the scenic road. The Gulf of Mexico was on the left, with hotels, restaurants, casinos, shops, and all sorts of businesses on the right. As they proceeded, the size and quality dropped. Finally, she turned into a parking place in front of a garish pink building with flashing lights surrounding a bright pink heart customers walked through to reach the front door.

They both sat quietly after she turned off the ignition. *She's too good for a place like this. She's probably regretting the whole thing.* "I saw several nice looking wedding chapels on the way into town," he said.

"I picked this one because it will be easier to get by the law . . . at least cheaper." She played with the strap on her handbag. "He'll point it out and say he can't marry us for three more days. You'll . . ."

"I'll say, 'Is there any way we can get around this problem?' and slide a bill toward him."

"Yes. You might get by with five dollars . . . ten at the most."

He pulled the roll of bills from his pocket and arranged it with two fives on top, rolled it again, and stuck it away. *I hope I can handle what I'm getting myself into—marriage to this woman who lives high and has secrets I can't comprehend. If it wasn't for Sarah . . .* He thought about the frail little girl who depended on him for everything. *I would marry the devil if it meant protecting Sarah, and maybe I am.* There were other alternatives but not if he wanted to stay close and be sure that justice was done.

Chapter 6

A few minutes later, they were a married couple. It was a simple ceremony. Dorie refused the rental of a bouquet of dusty flowers, a Victrola recording of the "Wedding March" or "I Love You Truly," and a photograph to commemorate the occasion, so the total cost came to fifteen dollars. Five was for the ceremony itself, five for ignoring the three-day wait policy, and five for agreeing to take the license to the courthouse to be recorded, fraudulently dated three days hence, of course.

"Let's get to the hotel," Dorie said as she got back into the car. "I'm beat."

"Would you like for me to drive?"

"Nobody drives my car but me." She sounded a bit testy.

"OK. That's fine by me." He wouldn't upset her over anything as trivial as driving her car. "What hotel are we headed for?"

"The Tremont. It's a fine hotel, better than any other in Galveston except the Galvez. We won't stay at the Galvez. Anyone I know who just might be in town would be there, so this cuts down the chance of running into acquaintances."

"I doubt we'd run into any of *my* acquaintances." The joke fell flat.

Back in the center of town, they pulled up in front of a four-story building, decorated in the style of the last century. Carvings and gargoyles protected the entrance. Valets came bounding out to take charge of their luggage and the many packages riding loose. Another valet took the keys and whisked the car away to an unknown location.

Jonah wondered about her 'no one drives my car but me' policy but knew better than to mention it. Walking across the magnificent lobby, Dorie took his arm and pulled him closer. "The reservation is in your name. It is for a one-bedroom suite for two nights."

They were accepted. Mr. and Mrs. Jonah Crandall. Husband and wife. No questions. No problems. No bribes necessary.

The suite was lavish. It had two big rooms—big enough to make twice that many normal-sized rooms. He'd never seen anything so luxurious. Not that he'd ever seen the inside of a suite in a high-class hotel.

"You can sleep on the sofa here in the parlor. I'll take the bedroom. You're probably hungry. You can order anything you want to eat, just use the telephone and ask the front desk for room service. They'll send it up. There's probably a menu somewhere. Sign the ticket that comes with it, and it will get charged to the room." He felt like a schoolboy being taught how to act.

"Tip the waiter who brings the food. I'm going to take a nap. I'll be up in an hour or so and order what I want."

She didn't wake up until the next morning.

He had been up since dawn, looking over the rooftops to watch the waves hitting the shore blocks away. He was spellbound by the color of the water as it changed from green to turquoise to navy blue. Far out to sea he could see faint silhouettes of ships and wondered where they were headed.

"Good morning." He turned to see his bride wrapped in a robe and hair standing every which way. "I didn't intend to sleep so long. I guess I was more tired than I thought."

"It was a long day, and you did all that driving."

"Yes, but I usually enjoy driving."

He shrugged. "Lots of tension yesterday. Lots to think about and get taken care of."

"Yes, there was, but we . . ." Suddenly her face became pale, and she turned and rushed from the room. The suddenness of her movements frightened him, and he followed her to the door of the bathroom that opened into her bedroom. The sound of her emptying the contents of her stomach reached him through the partially open door.

When it stopped, he asked, "Can I help you in any way?"

"No . . . no, thank you." He heard the flush, then water running in the sink and splashing. She came out, her color returning to normal. "It was all the heat yesterday, I think, and all that driving. I should have had the top up, but I like the air blowing when it's down."

"You didn't have any supper last night—nothing after the sandwich you had for lunch. You need to eat something."

"You're probably right, but I don't know if I can keep much down. Maybe some toast."

"I'll order whatever you want. Why don't you sit down and take it easy?" *I'm getting to be an old hand at ordering from room service,* he thought. "Anything else besides toast?"

"Tea. Hot tea sounds good. I'll get dressed while we're waiting for that. Have you had breakfast?"

"Yes, about an hour ago."

"You must be bored just sitting around this hotel room."

"Not really. I've had a lot to think about, and the windows give me an ever-changing view of the ocean."

"It's the Gulf of Mexico, you know, not precisely the ocean."

"Close enough."

She smiled and went through the door to the bedroom and closed it behind her.

Don't pay any attention to that smile. This isn't real. This is play-acting.

Chapter 7

An hour later, they were walking along a section of town that Dorie called "The Strand."

"The actual name of the street is Avenue B, but that doesn't sound very special," she said. "So it is called The Strand, which means 'beach.' It used to be an active business district. You'll still see banks and wholesalers along here but nothing like it used to be."

"I assume the hurricane changed all that."

"You're right, the hurricane and the depression. Both devastated the area, but it's coming back. There are more retail stores now than there used to be. I wanted to see what is here these days."

Jonah walked beside her as they browsed the shops and businesses along the way. A bookstore, stationery shop, along with banks, title companies, and attorneys' offices lined the busy street. Finally, Dorie entered one of the shops.

A leather goods store gave forth the aroma of expensive goods. To Jonah, it smelled like a saddle-maker's shop, or maybe a bootmaker. He wasn't far wrong, except in the more urban atmosphere, the footwear was shoes, not boots. A salesman approached as soon as they entered. "May I help you?"

"Yes," Dorie said. "I'd like to see some luggage."

"Certainly, madam. This way."

She picked out a valise and a suit bag, very expensive and very masculine in style. "Madam has good taste," the salesman approved.

"You can have these delivered to the Tremont this afternoon." It wasn't a question. She gave him the suite number.

As they left, she said, "You needed something to put your new wardrobe in. We can't be carrying your clothing around in paper wrappings."

Jonah said nothing, but the feeling of being a kept man was getting stronger by the minute. *This is all for Sarah,* he kept telling himself. *She'll have a safe home, at least for a year, and plenty to eat. I can put up with it for that long.*

"I'm hungry," Dorie said. "I usually have a big breakfast . . . at least until this heat spell hit I did. There used to be an excellent place to eat overlooking the bay. Let's see if it's still here."

It was. The hostess showed them to a table for two next to a large window where they could observe the boats trafficking Galveston Bay. Commercial fishing craft were surrounded by hordes of seagulls hoping to make off with some of the catch. Larger ships made their way slowly on the path to exit the bay into the Gulf and do business up or down the coast. Small boats, manned by lone fishermen, worked among their bigger brothers. Occasionally a dolphin could be seen playing among the waves.

Their order made, Dorie asked, "Are you enjoying Galveston, the little bit you have seen of it?"

"Yes, I am, but I have a question."

Her eyes took on a shaded look, and her body tensed. It was obvious she expected him to ask something she didn't want to tell—something about this mysterious marriage arrangement.

"You know a lot about Galveston—its past, the businesses, where to go. How do you know so much about it?"

She relaxed. "I used to come here often with my father . . . with my family."

"Your father? That was Big Barnett, right? As in Big B Ranch?"

"Yes. Bigelow Barnett. Everybody called him Big B. He was a legend in the county."

"I've heard of him, and I'm not from around here. What about the rest of the family?"

She twisted the wedding ring on her finger as she stared out the window at the passing boats but said nothing.

"If you don't want to talk about them, that's all right. I don't mean to pry."

"That's OK. If we are going to pull this off, make people believe this is a real marriage, you'll obviously need to know something about me. Let's start with my family." She put her hands in her lap and looked directly at him. "There was my mother, of course. She was devoted to my father, and he to her. He had an outgoing personality, as anyone who knew him would attest to. He rather overwhelmed my mother. Outshone her, if you will. She was always in the background. That's where he thought women ought to stay, so she did, but she didn't mind that. She was content running the house and seeing to her husband and children."

The waiter brought two tall glasses of iced tea and placed them on the table.

"Do you have siblings?" He turned his attention to stirring the tea so as not to be looking directly at her. *Perhaps this subject is what is causing her tension.*

"I had two brothers."

"Had?"

"Yes." Again she sat silent.

He wouldn't push her. He let a minute go by before he asked, "Are they both dead now?"

"Yes." A long pause. He sensed that he'd have to pry a bit to find out anything more.

"What happened?"

"The war. The war happened." She stared out the window, lost in thought. Finally, she turned back to him. "They were both older than I. Bix was the oldest—Bixby. It was Mother's maiden name. He was Big B, Junior. It was Father's plan that

Bix take over some of the businesses when the war was over, when he came back home. It was Father's plan, understand, not Bix's." She sat in contemplation of the past.

"And he didn't come back?" he finally asked.

"Oh, he came back, but not the same man who left us." She played with the silverware on the table as she picked up the story again. "My other brother was Daniel—Danny. He was three years younger than Bix. Father always overlooked him in his quest to have another Big B running Barnett Ranch and Enterprises. Danny tried and tried to prove his worth. He actually wanted to put up with all Father's schemes and plans and business manipulations. He would have been the ideal successor, since he was as driven as Father and knew darned well how everything worked as well as Father did, too. Bix didn't want it. Didn't want anything to do with ranching or cotton warehouses or business investments—none of it. He wanted out."

She took the slice of lemon from the side of the glass, squeezed it into her tea, and stirred it.

"Then the war came. They had an agreement between them, Bix and Danny. When they came home, Bix would tell Father, tell him he was leaving. He was going to some big city, maybe Chicago or New York, and see if he could get a job at a newspaper. He wanted to write, you see, write about what was going on in the country and in the world. And Danny wanted to run Big B—the whole shebang."

"What happened to the plan?"

"Danny was killed in France. Bix came home . . . but not the Bix who left. He started drinking. I think he was trying to build up the nerve to tell Father he was going to go be a writer, but how could he? How could he leave Father with no heir for the businesses? He couldn't. And he missed Danny. He felt guilty for surviving when Danny had died. So he drank. And drank. And died."

"What about you?"

"No one noticed me, trailing along behind my two older brothers, adoring both of them, listening in as they made their plans, and watching how the ranch was run. Listening to conversations about buying and selling, storing cotton for the farmers, renting buildings, making deals, and"—she looked up at him and smiled—"how you bribe a person. No one realized I was learning, too, along with the boys."

"And then you were the only one left, and your father had no one else to turn to."

"Not exactly . . ."

"Dorie Barnett! Is that you?" The couple who approached their table, trailed by a hostess with menus in her hands, were a few years older and well-dressed. The woman was a bit overdressed for a vacation destination. She was wearing pearls and gloves, when the women Jonah had seen in Galveston were definitely attired more casually. "Homer! Look! It's Dorie!"

The bald-headed man accompanying her smiled at Dorie. "What a surprise finding you here in Galveston. Trying to get away from the heat, like us, are you?" The couple looked from Dorie to Jonah and back again, curiosity obvious on their faces.

Dorie took a deep breath. It had started. "Edna, Homer, I'd like to introduce you to my husband, Jonah Crandall."

Chapter 8

At that moment, the waiter arrived with a large tray bearing their food, forestalling any further conversation, and the hostess, who had been hovering in the background, took the opportunity to usher the couple to a table across the room.

"Your secret is out now," Jonah said as he spread the white linen napkin across his lap.

"I knew it would be. I *wanted* it to be. I just didn't think it would be this soon, and in this way. It's taken a burden off me—how to let the community know."

"Who are they?" He took a bite of the fish she recommended he order.

"The Malloys. He owns the hardware store in Cottonport and is president of the school board. Edna is president of the Cottonport Garden Club. When they get back home, the news will be all over town within an hour."

"And you don't mind that?"

"Not a bit. It's easiest this way."

"They keep looking this way. Smile once in a while so they'll think you're happily married."

She smiled at him. "Who's to say I'm *not* happily married?"

He shrugged and continued eating. "I'm glad you suggested this meal. I'm not familiar with seafood. This is good."

"I like grouper, too. I always get it when I'm near the coast so it will be fresh. What were we talking about?"

"You were telling me about your family, but I think we'd better continue that conversation some other time. It doesn't sound like the rest of it is going to be a happy story, and we don't want the Malloys to get the impression you are unhappy."

"You're right. There are some unhappy parts to the Barnett saga. They are better left until later."

After they finished eating, they made their way back to the hotel. The day had become hot, and the room was a cool oasis. "I'm going to take a nap," Dorie told him. "I don't know what's wrong with me lately to cause me to sleep so much."

He grinned at her. "Getting married is exhausting work!" Then he sobered. "Worn out from working the ranch and taking care of whatever this business is that caused you to marry me, probably."

"I guess so." She smiled back. "I hope you aren't too bored."

"I got a couple of newspapers at the stand as we passed. I'll stay busy reading them."

A couple of hours later she was up. "I'm going downstairs to the beauty salon and indulge myself. There's a barbershop, too. Why don't you treat yourself to a haircut and the works? Use that money I gave you."

"Are you telling me I need a haircut?"

"Yes."

"Fair enough." *When I agreed to this crazy marriage, I guess I signed up for more than I realized. She's bought me. She's still the boss, and I need to do what she says.*

Late that afternoon they were back in the suite, cut and polished, looking and feeling refreshed. "We'll be going back home tomorrow to heat and dust and bawling cattle. Tonight we'll live well. I'm going to make reservations at the Balinese Room for dinner," Dorie said.

"What's the Balinese Room?"

"The most prestigious dinner club in Galveston. Wonderful food. Celebrity entertainment. Gambling. Liquor of any kind one might want. Most anything illegal you could ask for."

"How do they get away with it?"

She shrugged. "Money. Influence. I don't know. They just do. They don't call this place Sin City for nothing."

She started toward the bedroom door. "But this is one of the safest small cities in the country. Common crime is not allowed. No muggings, no pickpockets, no brawls. Nothing that would discourage tourists from coming and spending their money in the bars and casinos." As she left the room she said, "Wear your new clothes tonight. Call downstairs and have them pressed. You clean up nice!"

It was early evening when Jonah stood looking out the windows of the suite at the last sparkles of sunlight on the waves. Dressed in recently purchased trousers, shirt, tie, and jacket, he felt like a stranger to himself. Someone he had known, perhaps, a long time ago. Someone very different from the cowboy he had become.

Dorie entered the room from her bedroom, dressed for the evening. "Would you fasten this bracelet for me? It's impossible to work the clasp by myself." She held out a slender strand of what he assumed were diamonds. It matched the small, glittering gems in her ears.

"You look beautiful." He had never seen her like this before. The lavender dress she was wearing clung to her body until it almost reached the hem, where it swirled about her calves as she walked. The sleeves looked like wings, wide and fluttering. Until this trip, he had never seen her in anything but a plain, perhaps faded, housedress, or, if she were going to be riding out on the range, denim britches and a long-sleeved cotton shirt, much like a man would wear. It wasn't that she was unattractive dressed that way—he thought she was an attractive woman no matter what she had on—but she didn't stand out. She could have been any farm girl, not the owner of Big B Ranch, manager of multiple businesses in Barnett Enterprises. This Isadora Barnett looked like a different individual. She had a new haircut, short and wavy, that brought out every sunlit strand in an already blonde cap of curls.

"I thought we might as well enjoy one special evening. I think you'll like the Balinese Room. They have excellent food, and there will be entertainment of some sort."

A few minutes later, she pulled the Auburn in front of an ornately decorated pagoda that stretched a long way from the seawall out over the water. Valets hurried to the side of the car, and Dorie relinquished it to them. Entering through a big red door into a Tahitian-themed interior, their senses were bombarded by the smell of sandalwood, the sound of music from somewhere in the back of the long building, the sight of colorful fish and exotic birds, artificial palm trees lit with small white lights, and the ever-present sound of waves under and around them.

"We have reservations," Jonah told the maître-d'. "The name is Crandall." The tuxedoed man checked a list. "Certainly, sir. It will be about twenty minutes before your table is ready. Would you care to wait in the bar? Or perhaps in the gaming room?"

As they walked along the wild carpet of swirling tropical leaves, Dorie said quietly, "The table is never ready. They want everyone to gamble first and leave some more money with them."

The room farthest out over the water was abuzz with slot machines jingling away, the roulette wheels clicking, and tables with games of blackjack and poker. "This will be crowded with people later tonight. This is early for the dedicated players," Dorie said.

There was a throng around one of the poker tables. As they eased their way closer to see what was going on, Jonah saw that the crowd was watching two players: an older, dark-headed gentleman, with a pencil thin moustache, and his opponent, a woman. He was surprised. He thought poker was a man's game. The woman was dressed in a sky-blue dress, slim and form-fitting. Around her neck was a most unusual necklace, made entirely of what appeared to be Indian beads. It was ornate, with native designs in red, yellow, blue, and white. Pinning her brown hair back from her face was a barrette of the same design, and two feathers were sticking out of it.

"That's the Cherokee Kid," Dorie whispered to him. "Watch. She'll win."

The Cherokee Kid sat back, at ease, a small smile on her face. On either side, a few steps back, were two brown-skinned men. Young and muscled, they wore dark suits, white shirts, and bolo ties with beaded slides. Their jet-black hair was long and tied at the back with a strip of leather.

"Are those bodyguards?" Jonah whispered.

"Yes. She's very wealthy. She was kidnapped once when she was a child, so bodyguards go everywhere with her now. She always uses Cherokees for the job." They watched as her opponent laid down his hand. The Cherokee Kid laid down hers and drew the pot toward her. The audience surrounding her applauded.

"Why is she called the Cherokee Kid? She doesn't look Indian at all."

"Ask Annie sometime. She knows. The Kid's real name is Julia something. She has a big house just outside Rock Springs." Dorie turned away. "Let's go see if our table is ready. I'm getting hungry."

The large dining room buzzed with the conversations of a hoard of diners seated around white linen-covered tables. Bright murals of Tahitian scenes covered the walls, and the fake palm trees attempted to convince the diners they were in the South Seas. Jonah and Dorie were led to a small table with a good view of the band playing at the other end of the room.

"Do you like Chinese food?" Dorie asked.

"I don't know that I've ever had any," he said, looking over the menu. "I think I'd rather have a steak tonight."

"This place was a Chinese restaurant to begin with, before it became Balinese, and they have good selections, if you like it, but I think I'd like a steak, too."

The waiter arrived quickly to take their order. Although he offered a full menu of cocktails to accompany their meal, they both chose water. Jonah would have preferred a beer, but after Dorie's comments about drinking, he thought it was wise to stick to water for the evening.

"I don't know if you saw them," he said after the waiter left, "but your friends are seated across the room with another couple. I don't think they've noticed us yet, but they will."

"Yes, I saw them. The other couple are from Cottonport, too. I hope they don't try to get us to join them."

"No? I thought you wanted everyone to know about the marriage."

"I do, but I'm not ready to be bombarded with questions I might have trouble answering. At least not right now, all at one time."

"I have a suggestion."

"Yes?" She looked at him with raised eyebrows.

"You do want everyone to believe this marriage is the real thing, right?"

"Yes. Of course I do."

"Then we are going to have to act like a newly married couple, not like friendly strangers."

"Well, we are friendly strangers, but I get your point."

"We'll have to do a little acting. Play the part."

"How so?"

"A newlywed couple would never sit on opposite sides of a table, not touching." He reached out his hand and drew hers to the center of the expanse of white linen. "They couldn't bear to sit here looking at each other but not touch, even a little." He lifted her hand. Propping his elbow on the table, he placed his other hand over hers, sandwiching her slender fingers between his strong, tanned ones. Lowering his head, he placed a kiss on her knuckles, then, turning her palm up, he placed a kiss in the center and closed her fingers around it. "You see? Anyone watching will determine that I am well and truly besotted with you." He gazed into her mesmerized eyes. "They will have no thought that this is anything other than a real, honest, for love marriage." He ran his thumb over the wedding ring. "They will know, or think they know, that I can't wait to have you back at the hotel and make wild love to you."

Jonah smiled as Dorie stuttered, trying to get words, any words, to come out. Her cheeks turned pink, and he wondered if she was thinking about what making wild love with him would be like. Although she pulled weakly at her hand, he knew she wouldn't make a scene over trying to get away from his grasp. He figured it was important to her that her friends see her as a happily married woman, and she wouldn't do anything to destroy that image. He kept his eyes on her face as he kissed her hand again, a slow and lingering kiss.

The waiter arrived with their salads, and Jonah was forced to release her hand.

"I, uh, I see your point. Keep in mind, though, that this will not continue behind closed doors. This stops with the public performance," she said after the waiter had left the table.

"I'll keep it in mind," Jonah said. He smiled to himself, noting her still flustered appearance.

"It won't go any further than this," she said sternly.

"No ma'am," he said, and aimed his smile at her.

As they were nearing the end of their meal, Homer and Edna Malloy approached their table. "Say, folks. We have a large table and just the four of us. The Keltons are with us. The dancing is starting as soon as the band comes back from its break. Why don't you come join us?"

Jonah spoke up before Dorie could think of an excuse. "Mr. and Mrs. Malloy, we do appreciate the invitation. You'll understand, of course, that a couple on their honeymoon would want the time to themselves. When we get back to the Big B, we'll be surrounded with work and people and all sorts of things that will keep us occupied. Right now, we just want to be alone together." He looked at Dorie with such a steamy expression that even a stranger could see he was holding in the passion he felt for his new bride.

"Sure . . . er . . . see you folks back home then."

The Malloys left, and when they got back to their table, they reported to the other couple, "He can't share her, he said. They're on their honeymoon." Everyone tittered, and the men started making jokes about honeymoons and wedding nights.

"Who would have thought," Edna Malloy said to Grace Kelton, "that Dorie Barnett would go and get married at her age?"

"I figured she'd be an old maid for life," Grace Kelton agreed. "Who's the man she married? What did you say his name is?"

"Crandall," Homer Malloy answered for his wife. "Never heard of him before. Wonder where he came from?"

"What business is he in?" Bill Kelton asked.

"Don't know beans about him," Homer replied.

"He's as handsome as a movie star," Grace whispered to Edna.

"I wonder what he's like in bed." Edna twittered.

"Lon Grainger's gonna be upset when he finds out," Bill Kelton murmured to Homer.

"What's Grainger got to do with anything?"

"I don't think he wanted it known, but he was after Miss Barnett, or I should say, he was after her land."

"Oh?"

The ladies paused in their conversation and heard this last. "Lon Grainger wanted Dorie Barnett? He's so rich he could have any woman he set his sights on. What'd he want with a plain thing like Dorie? I mean, she's as sweet as can be, but not his type."

"I don't know about that. Just look at her tonight. She's not plain at all. She's plum good looking." They all looked at the other table, judging Dorie's appearance.

"It's not her he's so interested in," Bill said. "It's what she owns. Eighteen hundred acres of prime oil land."

"They've never drilled on it. So how does he know?" Homer asked.

"They've found oil on his land, and the experts say the field runs her way. They're gonna start more drilling on Lon's land sometime after the first of the year, and he wants it tied up before then."

"Well, he's too late," Edna said. "He should have courted her early. She picked herself a husband, and it isn't him."

"If we leave now, they'll just think we . . ."

"Went back to the hotel and went to bed?"

"Yes." She looked away.

"They'll think that no matter what time we leave."

She looked at the tablecloth and drew an imaginary circle with her finger.

"So, why don't we dance?"

She looked at him. "You dance?"

"Yes. You?"

She nodded. He stood and held out his hand. Taking it, she let him lead her to the dance floor. The band was playing "Night and Day," and he gathered her close against him, resisting when she tried to pull back. "Remember to play your part," he whispered in her ear. "A new bride wouldn't pull away."

He used his finger to tip her face toward his so he could nestle his cheek against her forehead. As the dreamy music played, he turned his head and kissed her lightly. If she berated him for it, he could always say that the Malloys were dancing close by, but truth be told, he only noticed them after he had done it. When that song ended, the band immediately started playing "Isn't It Romantic," and Jonah moved her a little bit closer to him, reveling in the feel of her body nestled against his. When the strains of "It Don't Mean a Thing If It Ain't Got That Swing" changed the mood to lively, he took her hand and pulled her toward their table. Taking a quick look at the check the waiter had left in their absence, he threw some bills on the tray, grabbed her hand, and said, "Come on. Let's get back to the hotel."

Chapter 9

They pulled into the shade of the oak trees surrounding the Barnett home the middle of the next afternoon. Annie was sweeping the big wrap-around porch when they arrived. She looked distinctly unhappy to see them. "So you went and done it," she said as they climbed the steps.

"Yes. You knew I would," Dorie said. "It had to be done. The alternative would be much worse."

"You got that right," Annie replied.

Jonah didn't have much time to ponder the meaning of the words.

"Bring the luggage upstairs," Dorie commanded and started up the stairway. She stopped midway. "I'm sorry. I didn't mean it to sound that way. I should have said, 'Please bring the luggage upstairs.'"

"That's OK. Obviously you have things on your mind."

She didn't answer but climbed the remaining steps to the wide hall that stretched the length of the big house. "Sit yours down a minute and bring mine down here. Please." She entered a room at the end of the hall. "Just put it on the bed for me, if you will."

He looked around at the place she slept, curious about whether she favored an austere setting that her at-home persona would indicate, or a feminine boudoir more appropriate for the woman she was the previous evening. The room he saw was somewhere in between. The bed he placed the bag on was covered with a white chenille spread. In the corner sat a comfortable-looking, overstuffed chair with a quilt in a patchwork of lavenders, pinks, and greens thrown across the back. On a table between the bed and chair was a stack of books and a lamp. A dressing table sat against the far wall, a large mirror reflecting the room. The room wasn't overly fussy or frilly, but one could definitely tell a woman occupied the space.

"Thank you," she said. "I'll show you to your room."

He followed her down the hall to the far end. *As far away from you as you could get me, isn't it, wife?* The room she led him to was fitted out in a more masculine style. It was furnished with heavy oak furniture, and the spread and drapes had geometric designs in earth colors. The large room, airy and bright, was by far the nicest accommodations he had had for a long while.

"This should do you," Dorie said.

"Yes. This is fine." Jonah sat his luggage next to the bed. "Could you show me where my niece will sleep?"

Dorie went back into the hall with Jonah close behind. "I thought this room would do for her. It used to be my room when I was growing up."

The room they entered was perfect for a girl: the bed was covered in soft pink with a lot of ruffles and lace, the wallpaper had tiny pink rosebuds, and braided rag rugs in pastel colors covered the wide plank floors

"It's perfect. She'll love it, I'm sure."

"My parents were trying to turn me into a sweet little girl who didn't take part in the rough life on a ranch. It didn't work."

No, it didn't work. You're out there with the men, working as hard as any of us, when you're needed. But somewhere inside, that feminine side lives on. I saw it.

"If you don't have anything you want me to do, I'd like to go fetch her now, if you don't mind."

"As I said, you can set your own schedule. That's part of our bargain."

"But if you need me, call on me."

"Yes. Yes, I will."

"Where will I find my truck?"

"It's in the small barn behind the house. That's where I keep the Auburn and my truck. You can keep your truck there, if you want, to keep it out of the weather."

"It's been in so much weather already that more won't hurt it."

Half an hour later, he pulled up in front of the small house he had visited a few days previously. As he mounted the porch steps, he heard the sound of crying and a strident voice coming from inside. "You snivelin' little whelp! Stealin' food! You'll eat what I give you, not go takin' what belongs to someone else."

Jonah yanked the screen door open. Crossing the room in one step, he grabbed the woman's arm, where she had her fingers wrapped around Sarah's thin one. "Let her go before I break your arm," he demanded. He shoved her away from the child, holding himself in check before he threw her into a wall. "How dare you touch her?"

"I shoulda known not to take a bastard into my home. This here's a God-fearing home, and I don't put up with no thievin'. She comes from bad blood, she does. Her mama was a whore, and she'll grow up bad, too!"

It was all Jonah could do to keep from striking the woman. He picked up the crying child and held her close to him. "Shh. Shh. It's going to be all right." He looked at the woman, venom in his eyes. "You won't have to put up with her any longer. I'm taking her with me now."

"Don't think I'm goin' to give you any money back. You done paid for this month, and you ain't getting any of it back."

"I wouldn't touch any money you've had your hands on." He threw the words at her. He entered the door to the side and started down the hall for the room he had been told would be Sarah's when he first placed her in what he had been assured would be a loving, homelike atmosphere. When he entered the room, he saw a perfectly made bed, and by it, in the corner, a blanket and pillow. Puzzled, he asked, "Where do you sleep, Punkin?" She pointed to the blanket on the floor. "Why don't you sleep in the bed?"

"I wet the bed one time, and she wouldn't let me sleep in it anymore." Her voice trembled and choked. Jonah held in the words that threatened to come spilling out.

"Where is your suitcase?" Sarah pointed under the bed. He sat her down and pulled out the cardboard grip then went to the chest of drawers. Opening it, he found two pairs of panties, both full of holes. "Did she not buy you more underwear with the money I gave her?" Sarah shook her head. He gathered the handful of items that were in the drawer.

"I bought you two new dresses to wear. Remember? Where are they?" Sarah shrugged. "Did you wear them?" Again, she shook her head. Looking at the floor, she said in a soft voice, "I heard her talking. I think she sold them."

He picked her up once again, grabbed the flimsy suitcase in the other hand, and marched back through the house. "I ought to contact the sheriff about your actions," he said as he crossed the living room. "Mistreating a child is against the law." He didn't know if that was true or not, but he hoped he could put a little fear in her.

"Like the law would take the word of a roustabout cowboy with a whore's kid over the word of a God-fearin', church goin' woman."

He didn't bother to challenge the allegation, but stormed out the screen door, down the steps, and to the truck.

"You don't have to be afraid any more, Punkin. I've got us a nice place to stay—real nice." *At least for a year.*

Chapter 10

Dorie took a cool shower to get the road dust off. Slipping into a loose-fitting housedress, she would have lain down on her bed except she knew she would have fallen fast asleep, and she was sure that Annie was waiting for her in the kitchen.

Annie ignored her at first, kneading a ball of dough onto a floured cloth. Finally, she said, "This is the last of the June apples. If we want apple pie after this, I'll have to use dried ones from last year until the fall crop comes in."

Dorie didn't say anything, but went to the cabinet to get a glass for some iced tea.

"It's not gonna do any good, you know." Annie said, picking up a wooden cylinder and rolling out the dough. "You getting married won't stop that vulture. What he wants, he wants. And what he wants, he gets."

"Not this time. He's not getting me."

"It's not really you he wants."

"That's very flattering, Annie."

"It's your land, and you know it. Everyone knows it."

She took a long drink of the cold beverage. "I know it," she finally acknowledged. She watched as Annie rolled the wooden cylinder this way and that, pressing the ball into a widening circle. "Here, let me." She moved into the spot before the unfinished pie. Carefully, she eased the dough around the rolling pin and lifted it into a waiting pie tin. Lowering it slowly, she adjusted the fit until it was smooth, with no air bubbles beneath to spoil its perfection.

She reached for the blue bowl Annie had used for the mix of apples, sugar, and spices and poured the contents into the pie shell, using the wooden spoon to spread the mixture about evenly. Taking a small paring knife, she trimmed the excess crust, leaving about an inch hanging. Her fingers folded and crimped until the edge was uniformly fluted all the way around. The dough she had cut off, she rolled into a ball.

"There will be another person for dinner."

"You mean your husband? I done counted on him."

"Besides him. His niece is going to live with us. He's gone to get her." Using the wooden rolling pin, she proceeded to flatten the ball, shaping it into a long strip.

"Huh!" Annie carried a bowl of potatoes from the counter to the table, sat down, and began peeling them. Finally, she asked, "A kid or a grown-up niece?"

"A child, I think." She took the paring knife and cut the dough into strips. Laying them on the apples, she wove them in and out to make a lattice.

Annie admired the pie. "You always did like that part of making a pie, even when you was a little girl."

Dorie took her glass of tea and sat in one of the kitchen chairs drawn up to the big table. Annie kept glancing at her. "Out with it, Annie. What do you want to say?"

"Are you sure the niece is not some woman, his piece on the side?"

Dorie studied on that a minute. "No. I'm not sure." She got up, went to the refrigerator, and poured more tea into her glass. "But if it turns out to be, she won't stay here."

Annie nodded her head. "That's good." She picked up the pie and slid it into the waiting oven.

"But I'd be surprised if that is the case."

"Don't never be surprised at what a man will do."

When Jonah walked into the kitchen an hour later carrying a thin, dirty, bedraggled girl, both Dorie and Annie were not only surprised, but appalled.

"This . . . this is your niece?" Dorie asked. Her hands fluttered in helplessness.

"*Edoda!*" Annie murmured.

"Yes. This is Sarah." The girl turned her head a little to peek at them as she continued to cling to his neck. "When I got to where I was boarding her, conditions were even worse than I had thought."

"I . . . what can I do? What does she need?" Dorie went forward. "Hello, Sarah," she said. She reached out her hand but hesitated to touch the child. She didn't want to frighten her more than she already was. "My name is Dorie." She pointed. "And that is Annie. We're happy to have you come live with us." She turned toward the Indian woman for assurance. "Aren't we, Annie?"

"Yes, ma'am. We surely are plum glad to have you staying with us." Annie stood in front of the sink, twisting a dishcloth in her hands.

Dorie looked at Jonah. "What can we do?"

"I'd like to show her where her room is and then maybe . . . a bath. Could you help with that?" He paused. "I'm not sure it would be appropriate for me to give a girl child a bath."

"Of course! Come, Sarah." She smiled at the child. "Let me show you to your room, and then we'll get you clean." She led the way to the stairs and noticed the girl pulled her head away from Jonah's shoulder enough to look up the steps. She didn't appear to be frightened, so Dorie asked, "Have you ever been in a two-story house before?"

Sarah shook her head and loosened her hold on her uncle just a bit so she could watch where they were going. *Is she curious about what is upstairs or frightened of what might greet her?* When they reached the upstairs hall, Dorie said, "The room you will be using is the one I used to sleep in when I was your age. It's very pretty. I think you will like it." She opened the door, and Sarah took in the roses on the walls, the rug by the bed, and the rocking chair by the window. Eyes wide, she looked back at Jonah's face.

"You'll be safe here. I promise you this is nothing like the place where you were. Dorie is sweet and kind, and I'll be here, too. I'm not leaving you to go to work like I did before. I'll sleep in the room next door. If you get scared, you can come get me any time you need me. I promise."

She stared into his eyes for a few seconds then nodded and hugged him. He felt the difference in the hug she gave him this time. The other hugs had been in fear. This one was for love.

"Would you let Dorie help you take a bath? She has a great big tub for you to wash all over in. Let me show you." He carried her to the room next to hers.

"Wait! Let me get something," Dorie said and took off for the other end of the hall. In moments, she came back with her hands full of bottles and jars. "I had to get some things we girls use when we bathe," she said and smiled at Sarah.

Jonah stood the girl on her feet. He kept his hand on her shoulder as he observed how she was taking in this new place. Squatting beside her, he said, "Dorie's going to help you get started with your bath. Is that OK with you?" She looked up at Dorie and nodded.

"I'm going to draw some nice, cool water in the tub," Dorie said as she leaned over and put the stopper in the drain. "I think you'll feel better when you get all clean, and the water feels good on a hot day like today." She turned on the tap, tested the temperature with her hand, and turned on the hot tap just a little to dilute the cold well water. "Let's put some bubble bath in. That's always fun!" She took the top off a bottle filled with lavender liquid and poured some under the running water. Immediately, bubbles started building up into a cloud-like tower. Sarah was watching, and when the bubbles billowed, she leaned forward, eyes wide.

"Time to take your clothes off and get in the water," Dorie said. "Can you do it yourself, or shall I help?"

"I'll leave you two girls to the bath," Jonah said. He stood and walked toward the door. "I'll be in my room."

Sarah looked at the bubbles one more time but made no move to undress.

"May I help you?" Dorie asked, and reached toward the hem of the ragged dress. Sarah stepped back out of reach and, grabbing a handful of fabric, pulled the dress up and over her head. It was all Dorie could do to keep from gasping when she saw the bruised skin stretched tight over her ribs. *Surely this child had not been fed enough to keep a bird alive, and the bruises! A child shouldn't have bruises!* She vowed to get to the bottom of the story. *Jonah acted like he was rescuing Sarah from a bad situation, but if he had any part in what had happened to his niece, then I'll . . . well, I don't know exactly what I'll do except protect the child.*

"Can you climb over the side of the tub?" she asked as Sarah pulled down the threadbare panties. "We may have to get a little step stool to put by the side so you can get in."

Sarah had no problem putting a leg over the edge and boosting herself into the waiting water. Settling into its depth, she sat still and looked at the bubbles that surrounded her.

"I think that's deep enough, don't you?" Dorie shut off both knobs. Going to a tall, white cabinet, she retrieved a washcloth and returned to the tub. "I'm going to put some soap on this," she said as she dunked the cloth in the bath water and took a bar of soap from a tin holder hooked over the side of the tub. "This is Camay soap. Doesn't it smell good?" She held it toward the girl. "I always think I smell good when I use it." She wondered if the child even knew how to take a bath. It looked as if she seldom, if ever, had one.

"Now, you take this"—she handed the cloth to Sarah—"and rub it all over yourself. All over your arms. All over your legs. All over . . ." She stopped when she saw the girl scrubbing herself vigorously. "Yes, you know how to do it!"

Dorie sat on the ladder-back chair in the corner while she watched Sarah clean herself. She was thorough, scrubbing elbows and knees, pausing occasionally to play with the bubbles, picking them up and spreading them on her arms. A smile touched her face as she wiggled her fingers in the suds. *Ah, yes,* Dorie thought. *She knows about bubbles and baths and being clean. She's reveling in the sensation of it, like it's been a long time.*

"Would you like for me to help you wash your hair?" Dorie asked. "That's kind of hard to do by yourself." She had been looking at the dark mass that surrounded the girl's head. So dirty it appeared to be black, Dorie suspected it was really brown underneath the grime. Probably matted, it was cut in a short bob, with ragged bangs covering Sarah's forehead. She hoped the child didn't have lice.

Appearing to think about it for a minute, Sarah finally nodded her acceptance of the suggestion. Dorie would have liked to have had fresh water for the next step but didn't want to upset the cooperation she was getting. *The next bath will be better. We may only be getting the first layer of dirt off, but anything is better than it was.*

"Can you lay down in the water so your hair can get good and wet?" She hoped Sarah wasn't afraid of lying back and letting the water come up near her face. She had been herself, when she was small. She still remembered the trouble her mother had washing her hair until she got old enough to do it all by herself. Sarah hesitated only moments before easing herself onto her back. Dorie used her fingers to separate the oily strands and work the water through it. "I have some special soap just for hair," Dorie told her, reaching for the bottle she had brought from her bathroom. "It will make your hair shiny and smell good." She worked shampoo into the dark mass, and the tresses began to come free from the tangles. It took sudsing two times before she thought it was clean enough. "You can sit up now." She put her hand behind the thin shoulders and eased Sarah to a sitting position. "We need to rinse it really well to get all the shampoo out," she told the girl. "If I turn on the water again, can you stick your head under? Or should I get a glass and pour water over?"

Sarah looked at Dorie, staring into her eyes as if judging more than what was being said. "I can stick my head under."

Those are the first words she has said to me. The first words she has said in this house! Dorie adjusted the water temperature then stepped back to let Sarah take care of that job herself. Sticking her head this way and that, she blew loudly when the water gushed over her face. Finally, she sat up and let it cascade down her back. "I'm through," she announced.

Dorie took a large towel from the cabinet. "Stand up," she said as she approached the tub. When Sarah complied, she toweled the dripping hair briefly then reached down to pull the plug, allowing the dirty water to flow out. She wrapped the Turkish cloth around the girl's shoulders and lifted the slight figure from the tub and onto the rag rug. She rubbed vigorously and quickly, absorbing the last of the water, then, before Sarah could object, she picked her up and went off toward the pink bedroom.

There, on the bed, was a pair of panties, worn so thin it was a miracle they still held together. Beside it was a dress of faded cotton. It had once been blue but was now gray, with tiny designs that might have been flowers at one time. Sarah snatched up the panties and put them on. "Don't put your dress on yet. Let me get some lotion." Dorie hurried back to the bathroom and retrieved the bottle she had brought from her room. "Here, hold out your hands." She poured a little into each hand. "Put this all over your arms and rub it in. Doesn't it smell good?"

Sarah wrinkled up her nose and nodded.

"Now, here, let me pour some more. Hold out your hands. This is for your legs and feet." Sarah complied, smoothing the creamy liquid all over. "Now you'll be nice and soft, and you'll smell like roses." This made Sarah smile. "Let's put on your dress."

Dorie held the dress above Sarah's head, open so the child's arms could go up and out, and the dress slid down into place. It hung loosely from her frame and exposed her knees. *So she wasn't always this thin, but she's grown taller.* "Sarah, how old are you?" Dorie asked as she buttoned the row of fasteners down the back.

"Seven," came the answer, as Sarah tried to smooth the wrinkles from the skirt.

I would have guessed younger! How small she is for her age! How pretty she is. Her hair is closer to red than brown, and her eyes are so unusual. Jonah's sister must have been a beautiful woman.

"Come, let's go get your uncle. I imagine dinner is ready. Are you hungry?"

What a foolish question, Dorie thought as Sarah looked up at her with shining eyes. *She's starving!*

Chapter 11

The kitchen table was set for dinner. Evidently, Annie thought the formal dining room wasn't required for family, and that's what they were now, a family. Dorie could tell, though, that special plans had been made for this meal. If it had only been the two of them, there would have been much simpler fare. Annie was presenting her cooking skills to the new family members, whether she approved of the situation or not.

The table was loaded with fried chicken, mashed potatoes, white gravy, pickled baby beets, and freshly picked green beans seasoned with sweet onion and tiny bits of chopped ham. What really gave her away were the yeast-risen rolls. On a weeknight. With no company. Yeast rolls that had to be mixed and risen and punched and shaped, and risen again.

Jonah had held Sarah's hand as they followed Dorie down the stairs. "It sure smells good, doesn't it, Punkin?" Sarah nodded.

"Annie is an excellent cook. Everything she fixes is delicious," Dorie stated.

Sarah's eyes lit up when she saw the bounty on the kitchen table. "Now, everyone, sit down," Annie said. "Let me serve this little one." She stationed herself to the side of Sarah's chair. "Most people, they would pile her plate high with food. Problem with that is, what goes in too fast comes back out fast, too." She put a spoon of mashed potatoes on Sarah's plate and reached for the gravy boat. "She needs to eat slow as she can manage." Next came a scoop of green beans. "Which piece of chicken you want, *Usdi Tsisqua*? You want leg? Wing?"

Sarah looked up at Annie, unsure what to say. She pointed at the leg that Annie had suspended from the fork in her hand.

"Leg? You want leg?" Sarah nodded. "Say," Annie demanded. Sarah stared at Annie. Annie didn't move. Finally, Sarah said, "Leg," and Annie put it on her plate. "Ah, yes. Good girl. She speaks." Annie took the big red and white napkin from beside Sarah's plate and spread it in the child's lap then went to the other side of the table, where her own place was set. "Next meal, you not be so hungry, and we try 'please' and 'thank you.'"

"Annie, she's been through a lot . . ." Jonah began.

"Yes. Yes. I understand, but she is strong, this little bird. She will be even stronger when she feels safe. She will be so strong she will learn to fly."

There was little conversation around the dinner table. Everyone was unsure of what to say. There were too many touchy subjects. By the time the apple pie was served, Sarah's eating had slowed. She no longer wolfed her food, shoving another forkful in as soon as the last was swallowed, but savored each bite she took. Her face showed the delight she experienced as she ate the small slice of pie Annie served her.

"You like?" Annie asked. Sarah nodded. "Yes? You like?"

"Yes," Sarah answered.

"Good. Maybe I teach you how to make, someday. I taught Miss Dorie how to make lots of things." She looked at Dorie.

"Yes, you did, Annie. You taught me a lot, and not just about cooking, either."

"I think I'd better take this one upstairs and put her to bed," Jonah said, observing Sarah's bobbing head.

"I'll help with the dishes," Dorie said, "then I'll go sit on the front porch."

"You," Annie said, pointing at Sarah, "take cloth from lap and wipe face and mouth. Put cloth by plate. Then go."

Sarah did as Annie instructed then slipped off her chair and followed Jonah.

"She did good, that little bird," Annie said to Dorie as they took the dishes to the sink.

Dorie was watching the setting sun turn the sky pink and gold when Jonah joined her. "Did you get her settled? Does a new place have her upset?"

"She was asleep by the time I got her settled."

"Oh!" Dorie stopped rocking and sat up straight. "I just realized, I didn't see anything for her to sleep in! I should have gotten something of mine for her."

"That's all right. I got one of my shirts and put it on her."

"What did she sleep in . . . before?"

"Evidently, she just went to sleep in whatever she was wearing." His tone was serious and his expression troubled.

"I have to ask . . . how in the world did she end up in such a terrible situation? Did you place her there?" Dorie knew his answer would forever shadow what she thought of the man.

"When I . . . I came to be responsible for Sarah, I didn't know what to do. I had something I had to take care of. I asked the pastor of the little church in the community if he knew of someone, a family, maybe, or someone who would board Sarah, take good care of her, until I could . . . well, do something different. He said there was a woman in his congregation who lived alone and could use the money. He vouched for her, said she was a good person and would take proper care of Sarah. I took him at his word. I was wrong."

"Did you not visit Sarah? See that she wasn't being cared for?"

"I thought she was mourning the loss of her mother. Mrs. Finch said she wasn't eating. I didn't know she wasn't being fed." He leaned forward and propped his elbows on his knees.

"You didn't know about the bruises?"

"No. I just saw them when I changed her clothes a few minutes ago." He shook his head. "When I got there today, I found she was sleeping on the floor because she had wet the bed."

"That's not so terrible. Probably a lot of kids sleep on a pallet on the floor, and some of them because they wet the bed. The bruises are something different altogether, and the hunger."

"That part of her life is over. I will never leave her again." Jonah spoke firmly.

"She will be safe here, and she will be especially well cared for with Annie watching over her."

"Annie seems a little bit . . . tough."

"Annie is wonderful. She started raising me when I was not much older than Sarah."

"Is that so? But you had a family."

"Yes, I did." She rocked a bit. "A family in name. But at that age, I needed more."

Jonah was quiet, waiting on her to explain, if she wanted to.

"I was younger than my two brothers. My father doted on the boys. They were his legacy—his sons. I was a girl. Girls were patted on the head and then ignored. Boys would inherit the ranch, the business, the Big B crown. A girl would learn good manners and be married off."

"But it didn't work out that way, did it?"

"No, it didn't. When I was not much older than Sarah, my mother became ill. It was her heart. She spent most of her time in bed, and Annie was hired to cook and manage the house. When I wasn't following my father or brothers, I was following Annie."

"Where did she come from? Where did your father find someone like her?"

"An Indian, you mean? Originally she was from Indian Territory, the area that is now called Oklahoma. There is a ranch in the next county, near Rock Springs—the Double T. It's a horse breeding and training business. People used to think the Double T stood for Travis Thacker, but really it was for Thacker and Tenkiller. They owned the ranch together, but folks those days wouldn't have done business with an Indian . . . still won't, for that matter.

"Anyway, George Tenkiller brought young Cherokee men down from the Territory to work on the ranch. One of them was John Runningdeer. He eventually went home for a bride, and that was Annie. They lived on the Double T for a couple of years, until John was thrown from a horse and killed.

"That's when Annie came to live with us. She saved me. What I learned about life, I learned either from watching my father do business, or from Annie. Both serve me well."

"I see. She's almost a mother to you."

"Exactly. So when I tell you to trust Annie with Sarah, I mean it in the best and fullest way."

They were each caught up in their own thoughts and sat, unspeaking, as the sun sank beyond the horizon.

"See the line of trees in the distance?" Dorie pointed. "That's the Brazos River."

"I knew we were close, but I didn't realize just how close. I've been working on the east side of the ranch these last few weeks since I've been here."

"When the first settlers came to what became Texas, they were about to die from lack of water. When they found the river, they named it *Rio de Los Brazos de Dios*. River of the Arms of God. I've always thought of it as God watching over me."

"That's a beautiful name."

"Yes, and the river is beautiful, too. But when the spring rains come, we have to move the cattle to higher land. It can take life as well as save it."

They sat in silence for a few minutes before Dorie rose from her chair. "It's time for me to turn in." She headed toward the front door. "Annie taught me something else," she said. "Something important."

"Oh? What is that?"

"She taught me how to love," Dorie said as she went into the house.

Chapter 12

"Mr. Grainger, Lon Junior is here to see you," the secretary announced.

The man behind the massive walnut desk finished writing before he answered. "Send him in." He continued what he was doing, ignoring the younger man who stood before him. Several minutes later, he looked up. "How much do you need this time?" He folded the paper in front of him and stuck it in an envelope.

"What makes you think I need money?"

"What else would you come to me for?"

"Maybe because you're my father, and I'm interested in how things are going with you—with the family business." The younger man was a picture of the older man in his youth. He had the same mane of auburn hair and the same air of superiority. He didn't have the brush of a moustache the older Grainger sported, and his eyes were pale blue with a circle of deeper color around the outside instead of the brown of his father's eyes. The younger man's arrogance was shadowed by a nervous appearance, a fidgeting of his limbs and darting of his glance, something that Lon Senior noted. That, along with the fact that his son couldn't look him in the face, was a sure indication that the visit meant he was in need of funds.

Pulling a file from his desk drawer, Lon Senior asked, "Have you knocked up another girl? Is that it?"

"No, I have not! If you really want to know, I have some information I thought you'd be interested in. Something you probably don't know."

"Since I know about everything that goes on in this town, I doubt it, but go ahead." He swiveled his chair away from his son so that Lonnie wouldn't see the glint in his eyes. It was entirely possible for the younger Grainger to have heard something of value, but he didn't want to look as if he wasn't on top of every person and every move made.

"Did you know that Dorie Barnett got married?" He took a seat across the desk from his father.

Grainger turned the chair with a jerk. "Married? You must have heard it wrong."

"Not according to Bill Kelton."

"What does Bill Kelton have to do with Isadora Barnett? And why were you discussing her with him, anyway?"

"I was in his accounting office on business, and he was telling anyone who would listen about seeing her and her husband in the Balinese Room in Galveston a few nights ago. Homer Malloy and his wife were there and saw them, too."

"So who's the husband?"

"Someone named Crandall. Bill didn't know him, said Homer didn't either. Their wives said they thought he was handsome."

"I don't know how that wallflower could get a man. She never goes out anywhere. How would she meet anyone, much less a looker?"

"I don't know, but she must have."

Lon Senior stared off into space.

"I guess this messes up your plans, huh?" Lonnie had a smirk on his face, and Lon Senior thought his son took perverse pleasure in seeing his father's schemes fall apart.

"It only slows them down a bit. It doesn't change the fact that I'm going to get her land."

"I had the idea you were going to marry her and take it over."

"So? She might not be married to him forever."

"They're young. They might be married for a long time."

A wicked smile appeared on the older man's face. "Or maybe not." He sat up straight, and a thoughtful look took over. "I need some more information about this Crandall fellow. Maybe he married her for her money. If he can be bought, he might be a valuable asset."

"And if he married her for love?"

"Only a fool marries for love." He picked up a pencil and twirled it between his fingers. "And speaking of that, how's your lovely wife?"

"Myrnalee's fine. Why?"

"Just wondering, son. Just wondering. She sure loves you. It would be a shame if she ever found out about some of your . . . well, let's call them your mistakes."

"Don't threaten me. I do what you want because it benefits us both. Whatever is good for Grainger Industries is good for both of us."

"And don't you forget that, son. Don't you forget that."

Chapter 13

Sarah sat on the bottom step to the porch, smoothing the skirt of her new dress. It was blue with tiny pink and yellow flowers scattered on the fabric. She loved to touch each flower with her finger and try to find the ones that were just alike. Miss Dorie had bought Sarah a lot of new clothes—dresses and panties and breeches and shirts. She had two nightgowns to choose from, and even socks and shoes to wear, if she didn't want to go barefoot.

She couldn't remember ever having that many clothes. Sometimes, when her papa came to visit and gave her mother money, Sarah might get a pair of shoes, especially if it was cold weather, or maybe a dress, but never both, and never more than one of anything, like now.

Now she had plenty to eat all the time. Not like when Mama ran out of food and money before Papa came, and not like it was at Mrs. Finch's house, where there was food to eat, just not for Sarah, but food for every meal, as much as she wanted to eat. And if she got hungry before it was time for dinner, Annie would give her a cookie or a piece of bread spread with butter and sprinkled with sugar. Annie always had something special for Sarah to eat. She'd say, "We've got to get Little Bird fattened up."

As she sat on the step waiting for Uncle Jonah and Miss Dorie to come back from the big barn, she became bored. They had taken her uncle's truck and gone to see about something Burt wanted to show them. Uncle Jonah asked Sarah if she would be all right at the house without him, and she said yes. She didn't want him to think she was some little kid who would cry if she was left by herself, but that was something she thought about often—being left all alone. Sarah had been all alone when her mother went into the woods and didn't come back, and she had been very frightened. Sarah cried a lot that time. She hadn't ever been scared of being alone until then. Before that, her mother was always there for her, and held her and rocked her when it thundered, and said things like, "I'll always be here for you, Sarah. Always." But she hadn't been. She left and never came back. It still made Sarah sad to think about that time, and sometimes she cried, just a little, when she thought about her mother.

Her mother had gone to see if she could find something to eat. "Stay here, Sarah. I'll go look for some fruit. I think there are some wild plums in the woods, and maybe some other things, too . . . wild blackberries are delicious. If anyone comes, you hide . . . you hear? Stay hid until I come back."

So when the two men came to the house, Sarah sneaked out and hid behind the woodpile. When they went inside the house, she crept up and looked through the window. They were pulling everything out of the drawers, like they were looking for something. They took the pictures off the walls and tore them up. They picked up the big Bible, the one Mama said had belonged to Grandma and Grandpa Crandall, and shook it before they threw it on the floor. Finally, one of the men said to the other, "We've looked everywhere. It's not here. Let's go," and they got on the horses they had ridden in on and galloped away.

Sarah thought that her father might come get her, but it had been a long time since he had been there, and she wasn't sure he was coming back. Her mother and father had a big fight the last time he was around. Mama wanted to move to town where she would have friends and could get food when they needed it, but Papa said no, she had to stay in the house he got for them way out in the country. Mama said that she might just have to figure out a way to get to town without his help, and Papa said she better do what he told her, if she knew what was good for her.

Mama wanted Papa to give her more money, too. She had to send the neighbor who lived across the fields to get groceries from the store, and the neighbor charged to do it for them. Papa said he gave her all he could, that she'd just have to learn to live on less, that he had expenses she didn't know about.

When Mama went into the woods to find some plums and berries, Sarah waited and waited, then the men came. When they left, Sarah waited some more. Night fell, and she was frightened of being all alone in the dark. She didn't know how to light the oil lamps, so the dark had moved in, with all kinds of scary sounds and shadows. When it was daylight, she was sure Mama would come back, but she didn't. Sarah thought about walking across the fields to the neighbors who bought their groceries, but she wasn't sure exactly how to get to their house. There might be wolves or coyotes or some other animal that would get her, so she stayed put. Two days passed before the neighbors came and found her, hungry and frightened. Mama never came back. The sheriff came and talked to her about Mama and Papa, and a few days later, a man came who said he was Mama's brother, her Uncle Jonah, and he took her with him.

Sarah thought about whether it would have been worse to be all alone with no one to take care of her or to be with Mrs. Finch, who had slapped and pulled and hit her all the time. If Sarah were all alone, she would have had to fix her own food, and she didn't know if she could do that. She didn't know how to work the stove, and she didn't know how to cook. Even when she was living at Mrs. Finch's house, the woman didn't feed her all the time, and when Sarah tried to get some food because she was hungry, Mrs. Finch hit her and called her names.

She was happy most of the time now, though. Miss Dorie was nice, and Annie, too. She wasn't the least bit scared of them, like she was at Mrs. Finch's house. Sarah was sure neither one of them would treat her like that mean old woman did. Uncle Jonah was sure mad at Mrs. Finch, and now Sarah was beginning to feel mad, instead of scared, when she thought about her time under the woman's care. Mostly, she tried to not think about it at all.

Annie came out on the porch, carrying a metal dishpan and a peck basket full of some kind of purple beans that Twisted Elk had brought to the house. When Sarah had first come to live here, she was scared of Annie, who was big and gruff, and, above all, an Indian, but weeks had passed, and Annie hadn't done anything to hurt her. She wasn't mean to Sarah. Sarah had to help in the kitchen and use polite words and good manners, but she had to do that when she lived with her mother, so it wasn't hard to get back into that habit. She had tried when she lived with Mrs. Finch, but nothing she said or did satisfied the woman. Uncle Jonah left her alone with Annie sometimes, but he didn't stay gone long. Sarah was sure he would always come back for her, so she wasn't frightened any more. Even if he didn't, Annie and Miss Dorie were there, and they would take good care of her.

"Usdi Tsisqua," Annie called out. "Come help shell peas, please."

Sarah stood up and made her way to the end of the porch, where Annie sat, doing something to make the little round peas come out of their shell.

"Look, I show you," Annie said. Taking her thumbs, she popped the two sides of the shell open and flipped it over. A whole row of peas fell into the pan, and she put the empty shells back into the basket. "See? It is easy. When we get all shelled, we will go cook them for supper."

Sarah took a bean and tried to imitate what Annie was doing, but the shell wouldn't open. "See, try this side." Annie demonstrated again. "Look at this, one side is a little different from other." The peas fell into the pan. Sarah studied the pea in her hand. She could see one side was a little different from the other. Trying again, she had immediate success.

"Twisted Elk says he will bring us some okra to eat with these, and maybe some tomatoes."

Sarah gathered her courage to ask a question that had been nagging at her for weeks, ever since she had met the man who helped in the garden and around the house. "Why is his name Twisted Elk? Why doesn't he have a regular name?"

"When he was born, one of his feet was turned back. It was turned while he was in his mother's belly. The midwife, the shaman, the spirit doctor, they all try everything they know to straighten it, but it stayed that way. Then they say Unequa must mean for him to have this affliction. So they named him Ugvtsusti Awie, Twisted Elk. Twisted because of his foot, Elk because he is big and strong."

Sarah had watched Twisted Elk from a distance. He tended the garden behind the barn where the car and trucks were parked. He fixed anything that was broken around the house and moved things that were too heavy for the women. "Do you have an Indian name?" Sarah hoped this didn't make Annie mad.

"My Indian name is Aiyane. It means Forever Flowering. White people, they think it sounds like Annie, so that is what they call me."

"Aiyane," Sarah murmured. She looked up at Annie. "That's a pretty name, and Forever Flowering is beautiful." She quickly looked back at the peas she was popping from their shells. She had asked several questions, and Annie hadn't rebuked her, so she tried one more. "Why do you call me Usdi . . . sis . . .?"

Annie smiled. "Usdi Tsisqua. It means Little Bird. You are like a tiny little brown bird. Sometimes people don't notice the little brown bird in the bush, but it is there, listening, learning. It sees the secrets people have. It grows smart. You are that bird."

"Usdi Tsisqua, Usdi Tsisqua," Sarah whispered over and over.

"You're learning to be a Cherokee," Annie said. "That's the last of the peas. Come to kitchen with me, and I'll show you how to cook them. You help with supper."

Chapter 14

"Now stir real slow, so it don't go outside the bowl," Annie said as she poured bacon grease from the coffee can into the waiting black iron skillet. "Now shake some salt from this shaker into the bowl and stir some more." She handed over a ceramic rooster with holes in the top and adjusted the flame under the pan.

Sarah had pulled a chair over to the counter so she would be tall enough. She was stirring sliced okra into corn meal when Jonah and Dorie entered the kitchen. He had his hand under her elbow, and she was leaning against his side. He helped her to a chair at the table and eased her into it. "Annie, could you get her a glass of water, please?" He went to the sideboard and retrieved a cloth from one of the drawers. Going to the sink, he wet it, wrung it out, and took it back to Dorie. "I think you need to see a doctor," he said. "You kept saying it was the heat, but it's cooled off now, and you're still sick and dizzy. Something's wrong."

Annie put the water in front of Dorie. "It'll be better by and by. As soon as baby gets bigger, it will stop making her sick," Annie said.

Jonah froze and stared at her. His eyes opened wider, and his mouth dropped. He looked down at Dorie, but she had the cloth over her face, absorbing the cool moisture on her skin. "The baby," he said in a voice as cold as ice.

"Yes." Dorie said, and took the cloth from her eyes. "The baby."

He turned and left, and after a moment they heard the front screen door slam.

"He didn't know?" Annie asked.

"No. I hadn't told him yet."

"I think you better tell him the whole story. After all, you dragged him into this."

"I know I did."

"And the *tianuwa*, he will be around again, soon."

"Maybe not."

"The hawk, he does not give up. He will be back." Annie picked up a plate of sliced tomatoes and sat it on the table. "It will not be long."

"It's been weeks since he called."

"He don't give up, that one. He wait and watch. Just because when he calls you on the telephone I tell him you are out of the house, or asleep, or busy, that don't mean he will quit." Dorie didn't answer.

Annie went back to the stove and spooned the okra into the hot grease. "You did good job," she told Sarah. "You are cook's helper." A smile spread across the child's face. "Now we will put the peas into a bowl. I tell everyone you helped shell, helped cook."

When the okra was nicely crisp, Annie put it into a bowl with brown paper in the bottom to absorb the oil and pulled a black iron skillet full of cornbread from the oven. "Go," she said to Sarah, "tell your uncle to come eat. It is ready. If he say no, make him come anyway. Say to him that you cooked it. He must come eat it." She went to the refrigerator and pulled out a bowl of cantaloupe and put it on the table.

After supper, everyone helped clear the table. "You take your husband out to porch," Annie told Dorie. "Little Bird and I will wash dishes, then I will see that she gets clean in her bath and put her to bed. You and husband talk."

Dorie knew Annie was right. It had been long enough—too long—and he ought to know the whole story. He was entitled to know her shame. She had paid for him with her money, but he was paying, too, chained to a wife who wasn't a wife. She only hoped that he didn't pay with his life. The foreman, Burt, had told her there had been someone messing about on her land—someone who was staying hidden, only occasionally glimpsed by one of the ranch hands, but someone who had no business being on the Big B. When she heard that, it had occurred to her that she could be made a widow very easily, especially if Jonah wasn't aware that his life might be in danger. Even if he was aware, it might not save him.

The screen door squeaked as she opened it. Jonah was already in the chair he favored. Dorie had taken a shawl from the hall-tree on her way out, and now she pulled it around her shoulders. Daylight hours were growing shorter, and evenings were cooler. She took the chair next to Jonah's and tried to think of how to start the conversation. His gaze remained on the last rays of the sunset, and he remained silent.

"I meant to tell you before now," she said.

"Whose is it?"

"Jonah . . ." It was hard for her to say the words. "I know you have questions."

His voice rose slightly. "Yes, I have questions. Who is your lover? Why didn't you marry him? Oh, I know, he's married, isn't he? I need to know, so I don't make a fool of myself if I meet him. I—"

"I was raped." She said it quietly, speaking the words aloud for the first time.

He turned to look at her, and she thought that in that moment he looked as if he could have killed, and gladly, for her, this stranger he was married to. She was surprised by his anger, this husband who didn't marry her for love.

"Did you go to the sheriff?"

She shook her head.

"Why?"

"Because it would have done no good."

"No good?"

She shook her head again.

"I can't believe that. Surely . . ."

"No. He . . ." She lowered her head and cleared her throat. "He is an influential man. The judge is one of his best friends. He would have said that I was . . . willing."

"Who is it? I'll disabuse him of that notion." Jonah stood up and walked to the porch railing. "I'll—"

"You'll do nothing. You'll only make things worse."

"How can they be worse? Tell me!" He was almost yelling at her.

She looked up, looked him full in the face. "He doesn't want me! Not Dorie! He wants the Big B Ranch. He wanted me to marry him so he can get control of my property. He raped me because he thought I would be so cowed—so embarrassed—that I'd marry him because that was my only option!" *There! I've said it out loud to someone besides Annie. My shame is out in the open.*

Quiet fell over them. Jonah watched the last sliver of sun slide behind the horizon. "That's why you had to marry me in a hurry."

"Yes. Now the child will be yours. There's no way he can prove otherwise."

"Even when the baby comes too early to be mine?"

"It won't be that early. As soon as I realized that I was expecting, I started thinking about what to do."

"And you came up with marrying me."

"Yes." She sighed. "Don't worry. I'll never hold you responsible for the child."

A lightning bug blinked a few feet away and was answered by a friend in the bush by the porch. "Why did you pick me?"

She smiled. "The times I had conversations with you about the ranch and all, I could tell you were smart."

"Smart? That was important to you?" He stared at her. "Being smart is important in some areas of life, but I wouldn't have thought a woman would have intelligence as a requisite for marriage, especially when the man isn't needed for support."

"Yes. I couldn't have married a stupid man."

"Why?"

She sighed again. She had hoped she wouldn't have to explain why she had picked him. "Several reasons. One, I can't stand to be around stupid people. They irritate me. Two, we would have no way to interact with each other—to have conversations. It was . . . is important that I can converse with my husband, even in this farce of a marriage. I needed you to understand, when I explained my reasoning, why I am doing what is necessary. Some men would have thought I should marry the man who raped me, that it was the proper thing, the decent thing to do. They wouldn't understand my resistance. Three, people would never believe I would marry someone who isn't my equal."

"You think I'm your equal?"

"Yes."

"One time, you started to explain what a word meant. You thought I didn't know it."

"You . . . anyone can have words they don't know because they haven't heard them before. Intelligence is a lot more than what words you know, or don't know."

He returned to his chair.

"After we married, I learned what a kind man you are. You can tell a lot about a man by how he treats a child. You are kind and loving toward Sarah. That shows me who you are inside."

"You didn't even know about Sarah until I asked if she could come live here."

"I know. I had already made up my mind about you before that—picked you as somebody I could trust. Seeing you with your niece made me more confident in my decision."

She stood up and pulled the shawl more closely around her. "It's getting cool, and I'm sleepy. I'm going to bed." She walked to the front door and opened the screen.

"Annie says there's one other reason I chose you."

"Oh? What's that?"

"Because you're handsome." Dorie had the feeling he was blushing.

"Was she right?"

She went inside, closing the door quietly behind her, leaving the question unanswered.

Chapter 15

Lon Grainger was irritated. After becoming accustomed to riding in an automobile, he was now forced to travel by horse, something he hadn't done in some years. It was necessary, however, to meet in a place where he wouldn't be seen or overheard, and everyone in the county knew who drove the distinctive 1932 Cadillac he was so proud of. Now his custom-made boots were dusty, and a streak of dirt marred his creased trousers. He might look like a picture of a successful rancher, but far be it for him to actually work at it, unless one counted bookwork, and most of that was done by an assistant.

He slid from the saddle and, holding the reins, led his mount into the trees that lined the bank of the Brazos. This far from town, or even farms or ranches, no one would be about, other than the person he had business with.

A low whistle led him to the right, and mounting a low bluff overlooking the river, he saw the cowboy, squatting in the underbrush. "Get down low," the rough-looking man said. "Anyone riding by could see you, standing up like that."

"There's not going to be anyone riding by," Grainger spat. "Not out here in the middle of nowhere."

"Can't be too careful." Seeing that Grainger wasn't going to comply, the man stood up, so as to be on the same level as the powerful man before him.

"So what do you have to report?" the rancher asked.

"So far, we haven't been able to get anywhere close to Crandall."

"I'm not paying you for what you *can't* do."

"I didn't say we wouldn't be able to, eventually, but he stays close to home. He's always with his wife or little girl."

"Little girl? He has a child?"

"I reckon. They're always together."

"That shouldn't be a problem. He's bound to be by himself sometime."

"No, it wouldn't, but some of the help have been nosing around the place. I don't think they got a good look at me, but they found my tracks and tried to follow them. I've been taking it slow and easy. Don't want to get caught snooping. That might make it hard to carry through."

"Is that all you're doing? Sneaking around spying?"

"That's what *I'm* doing, but Pete got hired on the crew. That ought to get him closer to the target."

"He ought to be able to find out what's going on over there then. The crew is bound to be talking about the owner getting married."

"They are . . . especially since she married a cowboy who was mending fence one day and marrying the boss the next."

"What?"

"That's right. He was working one day, and no one had any idea he was sparking the lady, then, all of a sudden, they got married. Odd. Real odd."

Grainger thought about the situation. Dorie Barnett was a smart woman. She didn't do anything without a reason. *Of course! She thought she would scare me off if she married someone else. She thought I'd give up. Well, think again, sister! What I set my sights on, I get!*

"And when they came back from getting married, or their honeymoon, or whatever, there was this little girl."

"Anyone know how she fits in the picture? Is it his daughter?"

"Nobody knows. The kid stays close to Crandall, or else that Injun who keeps house is with her." His horse sidestepped, and the man moved, calming the animal. He looked around, trying to judge if someone was nearby. Reassured they were alone, he continued, "I thought you'd want to know about the kid. Might could use it someway."

"Maybe." Grainger's mind darted in different directions, thinking of a way to use this information to his advantage. He brought his attention back to the man in front of him. "Under no circumstance is the woman to be hurt in any way, understand? Do it when they aren't together. She's liable to get in the line of fire, otherwise."

"Yeah, you told me that already. I've got it, but that makes it hard, when they're always together. They sit on the porch in the evening, both of them, but the way they move around, it's hard to get a bead on just him, and I didn't want to take a chance. Also, it's getting dark earlier. Sometimes it's practically dark by the time they come out."

"No chances of hurting her, understand? You'll have to think of another way."

"I've got it, I said! This is taking some time, you know, and the money you paid to begin with is all used up. We need some additional funds to keep going."

"I paid you plenty! Half up front and the other half when the job is done. That's what we agreed on! And I paid you plenty for that other job."

"That's when you told me it would be quick and easy. 'Pop him,' you said. 'An easy job' is what you said. This isn't quick and easy." He spat on the ground. "And the other job was the other job. We did it with nothing to lead back to you. That should prove that we are good at what we do."

"No more money. Not until Crandall is dead." Grainger went to his horse and swung up. "And do it soon. I'm tired of waiting."

Chapter 16

The brisk days of autumn were growing shorter. The wind gave a taste of winter that would arrive before long, and it had cleared the trees of all but the last few orange and gold leaves that held on past their time. The fireplaces in the Big House had either glowing coals from earlier fires or the popping and crackling of current ones.

Annie and Dorie sat at a round oak table in the living room. Annie had an iron dog before her. She put a pecan in the mouth and pulled the tail down, and the nutshell cracked. She put the fragmented pecan in a large walnut bowl that sat in the center of the table. Sarah had enjoyed doing the job earlier, but since she tended to pull down too hard and smash the nutmeats into tiny pieces, she had been relieved of the chore. She now lay on a rug in front of the embers in the fireplace, looking through a Sears & Roebuck catalogue.

"This Thanksgiving is going to be different from last year," Dorie commented.

"It was just you and me last year," Annie agreed. "This year we got us a house full."

Dorie smiled. "Yes," she said quietly. "We do." She glanced at the child on the floor and the man in the easy chair, reading a book he had found on the office bookshelves. *In the midst of misfortune, there is happiness if you look for it,* she thought. *If this scene was what it appears to be—a normal family with a husband, wife, and child . . .* "Oh!" She put her hand on her stomach.

Jonah looked up. "Is something wrong?" He lowered the book to his lap, a finger in between the pages to mark his place.

"No. I . . . the baby kicked me!" She had mixed feelings about this child. When she was growing up, she often felt unwanted and unloved. To her father, being a girl made her useless, unable to bear the family legacy of manly virtues like his sons. Her mother, who had taken ill with heart troubles when Dorie was only a few years older than Sarah, loved her, but didn't understand that her daughter craved her father's approval. Dorie couldn't remember the exact words her mother had spoken, but she knew, without a doubt, that she was an unplanned child.

That made this pregnancy difficult to think about. As the result of a rape, of course the child was unplanned and unwanted, but she didn't want to think of a baby that way. It wasn't fair. It would be a real person, an individual deserving of love, no matter what its father was like. Dorie had started feeling the first stirrings of maternal love when she realized the butterfly twitches were a small hand or foot moving in her belly. This was going to be her child . . . hers alone. Her molester would never know it was his, and the husband whose name would be on the birth certificate would be gone even before the baby's first words were spoken.

Moisture in a log made a loud pop, and sparks showered like a fireworks display. Startled by the unexpected noise, Dorie was pulled from her thoughts about the baby growing inside her. She went back to separating shell from nutmeat. Jonah frowned, stared into the flames, then returned to reading, while Sarah continued looking at the pictures that had her enthralled.

"When will the package with the things we ordered get here?" Sarah asked.

"It won't be long now, I hope. You need your winter coat and boots." The warm dresses, slacks, and shirts Dorie had ordered would be a surprise. Before long, she would have to think about ordering Sarah something for Christmas. *I need to start gathering things for the baby, too: a crib, clothing, and diapers. Yes, this holiday season will be very different from last year, and the years before that. It's been a long time since there was a real family Christmas in this house.*

"I think I used to have a winter coat, a long time ago. It was dark blue." Sarah turned a few pages. "I don't think I ever had boots, though."

"What did you wear on your feet in the winter?"

"I had shoes, but they got too little, so then I just had socks, but they had holes in them. Mama carried me to the necessary and back."

Annie stopped cracking pecans to enter the conversation. "You didn't have an indoor toilet?"

"No. Mama wanted to move to town so we could have one, but Papa said no, we had to stay in the country."

This was the first time Sarah had talked about her life before coming to the Big B. Dorie glanced at Jonah to see if he was listening. He had lowered the book to his lap, and Dorie wondered if Sarah had confided all this to him when he gained custody of her.

"These days, lots of folks who live in the country have water and toilets and bathrooms inside," Annie said. "Look at us. We live in the country, and we have all the conveniences."

"Papa said it cost too much money. He said he couldn't afford it." She turned the page. "Look, Uncle Jonah! Look at these dishes. Aren't they pretty?" She held up the catalogue for Jonah's approval.

"They sure are. How much does it say they cost?"

Sarah bent over the page, studying the numbers. When Dorie found out the child had never been to school, she was appalled. All children, in her opinion, needed to attend school and learn to the best of their ability. Sarah was smart, Dorie recognized, and why anyone would keep her home, keep her from learning all about the world, she couldn't imagine. She guessed that Letty and Sarah lived where there was no school close by. In the condition Sarah was in when she arrived at Big B Ranch, it would have been devastating for her to try to adjust to a classroom setting at that point. Dorie was gently teaching the girl the alphabet and the sounds the letters make. As they went about the daily chores, Annie talked to her about numbers and adding and subtracting. *I need to find out what all she needs to learn to be ready for school next fall.* Then it hit her. *Sarah won't be here next fall. The year will be up, and Jonah and Sarah will be gone.* A heavy weight settled in Dorie's heart.

It was time to distract Sarah's mind from those memories that made her sad. Dorie would find the child deep in thought, sometimes with tears running down her cheeks. She would gather the slight figure into her lap, where Sarah would lean against Dorie's breast with a shuddering breath. Dorie was curious about the details of what had happened, but all Jonah would say about his sister was "She's dead." Dorie thought it best not to pursue the subject until she and Jonah were alone.

"I'll be glad when the package from Sears & Roebuck comes, too. I'm having trouble getting anything to fit around my waist." She had ordered several loose-fitting dresses and a pair of men's overalls to wear out around the barns. When the order came, she'd have enough to last the last few months.

"I think I'll send Twisted Elk to town to the butcher's shop for a nice, big turkey for Thanksgiving dinner," Annie said. "Last year a hen was plenty enough for the two of us, but this year we'll have a real Thanksgiving." She smiled. "And I'll make a list to send to the grocery man, too."

"I'll be glad to go for you, Annie," Jonah said.

"No. You stay here," Dorie spoke quickly. Looking up, she realized Annie and Jonah were staring at her. "I mean, I think you ought to let Twisted Elk go. He is so proud of being able to drive that truck you gave him that you shouldn't take away his chance to show off his driving skill."

When Burt acquired a newer truck, Jonah bought his old one for almost nothing. "Why do you want this old junker?" Burt asked. "Even your truck is in better shape than this one. I've been using it on the ranch for years, and it's about all used up."

"I'm buying it for Twisted Elk," Jonah told him. "It's a chore for him to haul stuff around the home place, and if he learns to drive good enough, we can send him to town when we need something, and he can haul the firewood up to the Big House with it."

Twisted Elk was used to making accommodations for a left foot that turned in a different angle than most, and it wasn't that hard to learn to use the gas pedal, clutch, and brake. He and Jonah spent hours in the car barn replacing parts, changing tires, discussing the different dials and gauges, the fluids that had to be watched, and all the minutiae the man wanted to learn about automobiles. He was a quick learner, and soon he was volunteering for any chore that meant he could drive the treasured truck anywhere, any time. Especially now that winter wasn't far off, it would be handy to be able to drive himself to his small house about a quarter of a mile away. He often gave Annie a ride to her cottage, although it was only steps down a path from the back door of the Big House. It was longer to drive than to walk, but Annie would say she was tired, and Twisted Elk would be close by so she could ask him for a ride.

Dorie was glad to have an excuse to keep Jonah from town. Since it had first occurred to her, the thought that being widowed would open the way for Grainger to press her to marry him was on her mind constantly. There was a very real possibility that the man would attempt to murder her husband. The fear that something would happen to Jonah terrified her, and not only because it left her open to her molester, but because she had become used to having him around the house. She felt good when she was with him. She looked forward to their nightly visits, sitting in the rockers and watching the stars. She remembered when he held her closely during the dances they shared in Galveston. She wished she could have thought of some way to get him to dance again, put his arms around her again. *What foolishness! When this baby is born . . . when the year is up . . . he'll be gone. Gone just like Bix . . . like Danny . . . like anyone who has ever loved me. But he doesn't love me. This is an arrangement, a bargain. A husband for me and a home for a year for him and Sarah. When he goes, so will she, and I'll miss another person I love . . . Sarah. I do love her. And Jonah? I can't love him. I can't let myself fall in love with him. I just can't.*

Chapter 17

Dorie and Annie spent the next few days planning Thanksgiving dinner. Annie called the butcher and ordered two turkeys, one for the Big House and one for the cowboys who lived on the spread. Dorie told Cookie to put on a big meal for the men, and she and Annie baked pecan and pumpkin pies for both feasts. Sarah was put to work carrying and measuring and tasting.

When Thanksgiving Day came, Annie put a tablecloth on the big table in the dining room and got the good china out of the breakfront. She didn't trust Sarah with the company dishes, but set the table herself, placing the silver just so beside each plate. She told Dorie, "Your mama taught me how to do this right. She was particular about where the forks and spoons went." When the time came, the newly formed family took their places at Annie's direction.

"Mr. Jonah, you sit at the head of the table, and Miss Dorie, you sit at this end. Little Bird, you set over there, and I'll set across from you." They all obeyed.

"This is the first real Thanksgiving dinner I've had since . . . well, in a long time," Dorie said. "After the war, after Danny and Mama died, and then Bix, Daddy said there wasn't anything to be thankful for, and Annie and I, we would have a little bit special dinner, but we sort of ignored that it was a holiday."

"I remember when Mr. Big was alive, after your mother died, if anyone said anything about it being Thanksgiving, he'd get mad and leave the table."

"That someone was me, Annie. It would just be the three of us. Bix wouldn't celebrate Thanksgiving after the war, either. He didn't even come to the table."

"And then when they were gone, it was just us two," Annie said. "But Mr. Big was wrong. There's always something to be thankful for. Even when times is at their worst, you can always find something to give thanks to Unequa, the Great Spirit, for."

Jonah carved the turkey, and the bowls of vegetables made their way around the table. Sarah was now trusted to serve herself. Since she had learned she could always have second servings, she took small portions the first time around, asking for more of her favorites later.

"When I was young, every Thanksgiving we went around the table and each person told something they were thankful for," Jonah said. "My brother was always thankful for the pie we were going to have for dessert, and my sister . . ." He stopped, unable to go on with what he was saying.

"I think that's an excellent idea," Dorie said quickly. She didn't know if mentioning his sister had made him emotional, or whether he regretted that he might have called Sarah's attention to the loss of her mother.

"I'll start. I'm grateful for having all of you here around the table this Thanksgiving. I'm thankful we're all together. I'm thankful for all this delicious food and for Annie who knows how to cook it to perfection. Sarah, what are you thankful for?"

Sarah's eyes opened wide as she looked at Dorie. She had never been asked anything like that before. She looked down at her lap then suddenly raised her head again and said, "I'm thankful for all my new clothes, especially this dress, because it's my favorite." She ran her hands over the brushed cotton of the purple plaid dress she was wearing and then picked up her fork. "And I'm thankful for plenty of food and not being hungry anymore." She put a bite of turkey in her mouth.

"I guess it's my turn," Annie said. "Sometimes, when things are bad, we don't think they ever gonna be good again, but we're wrong. Long time ago, I love a boy, and I think he love me, too, but he goes far away to Texas to work on a big horse ranch. He say he'll learn his job and come back for me, but I wait and wait. I think he has forgotten about me, and I'm sad. Very sad. Then he comes, and we get married in Cherokee ceremony, and he brings me back to Texas with him. We are very happy for two, three years. Then he tries to break a wild horse, but it breaks him. Breaks him to pieces, and he dies.

"What will happen to me? I think I will have to go back to my father's home in Qualls, where he will tell me I have to marry again while I am still young. He will pick a husband for me. But I don't want a new husband. I only love John Runningdeer, even if he is dead.

"Then Mr. Big, he needs somebody to come help with house, with Bix and Danny and Miss Dorie, and Mrs. Barnett. She isn't feeling so good, so I come. I find family who needs me."

Everyone had stopped eating as they listened to her story. "Then comes sad time for Miss Dorie's family. One son, he is killed in war. Other son, he so sad he get drunk all the time. Mrs. Barnett, her heart is sick. Soon, Mrs. Barnett, she die, and son, too. Mr. Big, all these deaths make him so sad his heart doesn't want to live any more. He dies, too. Only Miss Dorie is left, but she needs me. I cannot leave her alone.

"Everybody needs to be needed. Everybody. I am thankful to be needed. I am thankful for Miss Dorie. I am thankful for family."

Silence fell over the room. Dorie used her napkin to wipe the tears from her eyes. "Annie, I am thankful for you, more than you can know. I don't know how I would have survived without you. You are my rock."

"Miss Dorie, you are a strong woman. You will always survive." She looked across the table at Sarah. "Just like Little Bird is strong. She is already growing in body and spirit. She is learning not to be afraid. She is learning to speak up. She is learning to stand up for herself and be brave. When she is older, she will fly into the world, like a bird leaves its nest."

Jonah had been sitting quietly, listening to all that was being said. All eyes turned on him.

"I'm thankful, first of all, for finding Sarah, for having her in my life. I'm thankful for having this home, this welcoming shelter for the two of us. I'm thankful for you, Annie, for helping Sarah bloom the way she is." He looked down the table at Dorie, his gaze boring straight into her eyes. "And I am especially grateful to the Great Spirit for sending me to my wife."

Chapter 18

When the dishes were washed and the leftovers put away, the household settled into peaceful lethargy.

"If you want anything to eat later, you can get it yourself," Annie said before she went home to her cottage behind the barn.

Jonah and Dorie settled into comfortable chairs in front of the fireplace, trying to stay awake to read. Sarah had an old catalogue and a pair of scissors that Annie had given her. She stretched out on the rug before the fireplace, cutting out pictures to make a pretend home and family. She had a picture of a house kit that the company sold, and she was busily cutting out pictures of the furnishings to go in it.

When Dorie glanced up a few minutes later, she found Sarah fast asleep, scissors still grasped in her hands. "Time for bed, I think," she said as she rose to her feet. "Jonah, will you carry her upstairs for me? I'll get her into her nightgown and into bed."

Together they mounted the steps and worked to prepare the sleepy girl for the night. As they both reached to pull the covers up around Sarah's neck, their hands touched. Dorie quickly glanced toward the other side of the bed, where Jonah sat, his eyes on the sleeping child. When he looked toward Dorie, he leaned forward, as did she, and their lips met as if pulled together by a magnet.

Dorie pulled herself back. *What must he think of me? That I'm forward, that's what! I must control myself. This is only a business arrangement to him, and here I am, acting like I'm a silly schoolgirl, expecting a real relationship. Don't mess it up, Dorie!*

She stood and walked toward the door. Following her out into the hall, Jonah said, "I wonder if there is any of that pumpkin pie left."

"Yes, there is. I'll show you where I put it."

I could have just told him it is in the refrigerator, she thought. *I don't have to go downstairs and show him.* But she wanted a few more minutes with him before they separated for the night.

A few minutes later, they were sitting at the kitchen table, with steaming cups of coffee and large slices of pie. Dorie was searching for something to say, something that would take her mind off the kiss.

"Tell me about your sister."

Jonah smiled. He took another forkful of pie before he began. "Letty was special."

"You know, I've never heard you say her name before. You've always said, 'my sister,' but not her name."

"It was really Letitia, but we called her Letty."

"Letitia is a lovely name. Was she younger than you?"

"No. She was the oldest in the family—in years, anyway."

"Oh?"

"You see, she really was special." He used his fork and played with the crumbs on the plate. "There was a problem when she was born. The cord was wrapped around her neck, and she went without oxygen for several minutes. The doctor thought she was dead, but she finally took a breath and, well, she made it, but it damaged her."

Dorie had never given any thought to the things that could go wrong during a birth. She put her hand on her belly, as if to reassure the baby inside, or maybe to reassure herself.

"She was slow," Jonah continued. "Slow to walk and talk, Mother said, but she did it. She went to school and eventually learned to read and write, but arithmetic and history and any of those things was beyond her understanding."

Dorie's heart sank for the young woman who was Sarah's mother. *How did she manage to raise such a sweet young girl? I wonder if Letty's disability had anything to do with her death?*

"She was beautiful, even as a child, with long golden curls and deep brown eyes. My older brother, Thomas, and I stuck close to her. We wouldn't let bullies tease her, and we had to watch out for the boys, too, who wanted to take advantage of her. Tom and I both beat up our share of kids who wanted to make sport of her."

"Does Sarah look like her? She's going to be beautiful when she grows up."

"No. Sarah . . . she doesn't favor her mother at all. As I said, Letty had golden blond hair and brown eyes."

"Like you."

"Yes, like me."

Dorie started to say, "She must take after her father," but not knowing the situation, she stopped herself before she blurted it out.

"When Letty grew to the age when most young women have a suitor, she could have had her pick, but my parents were adamant. She would not be able to manage a household, nor raise a child, without help. If Letty married at all, it would have to be to someone who understood this and was wealthy enough to hire a housekeeper and a nurse or governess to care for a child. Father discouraged any man who came around Letty. Of course, most of the families in town already knew about her problems, so that made it easy. No one wanted Letty in their family, anyway, for fear she might have a child with the same handicap."

"But that wasn't something that was inherited!" Dorie was incensed. "It was an accident, the cord being around her neck like that!"

"No, but people are fearful, and they don't always understand things."

Dorie wanted to hear how Sarah came about, but she didn't want to pry. As they ate their pie, she hoped Jonah would continue Letitia's story.

"One day, a new young man came to town to do business with my father. We lived near Waco, and my father had his hands in a lot of businesses: cattle farming, cotton, banking, and so forth. Letty and Mother happened by his office at the bank that day, and Letty was instantly smitten.

"He was charming, all right. I'll give him that. He said all the right things, and Letty listened. Father warned him off, but it didn't do any good. At the end of two weeks, he and Letty ran off together."

"Oh, my! I imagine your parents were worried."

"Yes, very worried. They had talked to him about Letty being slow, but they didn't know if he really understood what they were saying, and they didn't know him well enough to know if she would be safe with him."

Dorie got up, went to the stove, and turned on the burner under the coffee pot. "Did they come back, eventually?"

"Yes. They came back three weeks later. Married, they said, and Letty had the marriage certificate to prove it. Father was afraid Letty had been tricked into a sham marriage, but the license looked official.

"Her husband said he had to go home and break the news to his father—his mother was dead, I think—then he would be back to get his bride."

Dorie folded a dishcloth to make a thick pad and picked up the simmering coffee pot. She went to the table and refilled their cups. "I would have thought he would have taken his new wife home with him."

"That's what we thought, too, but that's not what he did. And he stayed gone a long time, a lot longer than it ought to have taken just to break the news. Letty said he was probably getting them a house fixed up to live in. She said he had told her he was going to buy her a real pretty house to be all hers. She was so excited about it."

He took a sip of his hot coffee. "By the time he returned, it was obvious that Letty was expecting. He only stayed a few days, said he had to go do some business for his father. And that's the way it went for four years."

"Four years? You mean he came and went for four years?" Dorie was astounded.

"That's right. Letty was as happy as a bug to see him when he came. She never asked why they weren't living together as man and wife. She never asked him anything. When Father ranted and raved about it, she cried, and then he'd settle down. Mother was happy that Letty and Sarah were home so she could watch after them. Letty could never have managed a baby alone. To Letty, it was like playing house, only with a real baby. When she wanted to stop playing, Mother took over.

"In a way, it was the perfect situation. Letty was still under Mother and Father's care, so that made them happy. She had a so-called loving husband who brought presents and showed up every few months to fawn over her. She had a baby to play with, a baby who Mother tended to. But, finally, Father had enough."

"What did he do?"

"Had a long talk with the so-called husband. Said he had to provide for his family. To tell the truth, without that marriage license, we would have doubted they were really married, but we had seen the proof. Father said if there wasn't going to be a real marriage, there would be a real divorce and child support."

"So what happened?"

"He arrived one time and said he had it all worked out. He had bought a house and was taking his wife and child to their new home. They packed up all of Letty and Sarah's things and left. We didn't hear from them for months, and Mother was beside herself with worry."

"I imagine so!"

"Finally, a letter came. It didn't have a return address on it, but Letty said she was fine and that she loved her new house, called it as cute as a dollhouse. She said it wasn't in a town, but in a beautiful area with lots of wildflowers. Sarah was doing fine, and growing, Letty said. Her husband continued to come and go, 'traveling on business' is what she called it."

"It sounds like things were working out. Were they?"

"Not by a long shot. Seems that he would bring gifts when he came and leave money for food, but Letty had no way to get to town. The nearest neighbors were about a mile away, and she had no type of transportation and no telephone. They checked on her every few days. She had to send for them to get food from town, and they mailed the letters to us for her. She was desperately lonely, and then the last letter came, the one that scared us to death."

"What happened?"

"He had stopped coming. Letty was almost out of food. She had taken Sarah and walked to the neighbor's house. She asked Mother to please send some money—said they were hungry and she owed the neighbors for the little food they did have, but she couldn't keep asking for help. She didn't know where her husband was, or if he'd be back."

"Oh, my goodness! That's terrible. Sarah had mentioned being hungry, but I never dreamed it was anything like this."

"That's when I started hunting for her. Remember, we didn't know exactly where she was. I had the postmark on the envelope, and I went there. Mother had sent mail to Letty and just addressed it to General Delivery. The neighbors would pick it up when they were in town. It was a little town south and east of here, just a wide spot in the road. Have you ever heard of The Thicket?"

"Yes. Isn't that the forest land, woods, marsh, bad lands, whatever you want to call it, that's spread over several counties not far north of Beaumont?"

"That's it. It's as wild as you'll find in the state, full of wild animals and wild men, too. A criminal, if he knows the area good enough to survive in The Thicket, can hole up forever, and the law can't find him. A woman or child would have no chance of survival in there."

"And that's where Letty was?"

"Yes. The house was at the edge of The Thicket. That's where she went to find food."

"Oh, my. Poor thing."

"Letty didn't stand much of a chance of coming out of a place like that. There are bears and panthers, and the place is swarming with cotton-mouthed moccasins. I went to the post office where her letters had been mailed, but no one there had seen or heard of her. Finally, the postmaster remembered the people who mailed the letters for Letty and told me where they lived. I went there and found Sarah with them. She had told them her mother went into the woods to find berries and plums for them to eat . . ."

Dorie gasped. *Poor Sarah . . . poor Letty.*

"They had gone to the house a couple of days before and found Sarah alone and frightened . . . and hungry."

"My God! The poor child."

"The sheriff, the neighbor, and I went into the woods to look for Letty. I knew what I would find, but it was worse than I thought."

"Worse?"

"She had been shot. Murdered."

Dorie covered her face with her hands. Tears made a track down her fingers.

"It gets worse."

She took her hands down. "How? How can it be worse?"

"Sarah said her mother told her that if anyone came, for her to hide and not come out. Two men came and searched the house. Sarah was hidden outside. They ransacked everything. The house was a wreck. I'm sure they were the ones who killed Letty. They would have killed Sarah, too, if they had found her."

"But why would they have torn up the house?"

"Looking for something, would be my guess."

"But what?"

"The only thing I can figure is they were looking for the marriage license. They were doing away with all signs of the marriage—license and wife—and if they had found the child, she would be dead, too."

Dorie was too stunned to speak. Her heart was fluttering in compassion for poor, dead Letty and the frightened child left behind.

"What . . . what are you doing here? In this area?" Dorie asked hesitantly, once her sobs quieted to where she could speak.

"Because the man behind all this, Sarah's father, is from here, from Cottonport."

Her mind churned with thoughts. "Who is it?"

"I won't tell you. It might make you act differently toward him—if you know him, that is."

"You're darned right it would make me act differently toward him!" She was incensed. "He needs to go to jail! He needs to be hung!"

"Of course he does, but first I have to prove things."

"Prove things?"

"That they were legally married, for one thing. That he was behind Letty's murder, for another. The marriage is the reason for the murder."

"So where's the marriage license?"

"I don't know. I can't find it."

They both returned to their cups of coffee, deep in thought about where the missing paper might be.

"You looked all over that house they lived in, I assume."

"Yes. I went over it thoroughly. It's not there."

Another thought occurred to her. "Why are you keeping Sarah with you? Why don't you take her to her grandparents?"

He grimaced. "I guess I should, but I want her with me. I know that she's safe with me. My parents' house would the first place someone would look for her. I can keep her hidden away as long as she's with me and no one else knows where she is.

"I thought I had her safely stashed with Mrs. Finch, until I found out how she was being treated. I can keep her here, with me, and watch out for her. That's why I don't want her going to town."

"Because her father might see her and take her?"

He snorted. "It's not likely, as little attention as he paid to her, but yes, that's possible. She looks so much like her father that anyone seeing her might figure it out. And he has reasons for not wanting anyone to know about her."

"What reasons?"

"He got married about two years ago. A marriage that isn't legal, since he was married to Letty at the time."

Her eyes widened. The story was getting worse with the telling. "And that's why they wanted the marriage license!"

"Yes. They wanted to destroy it. Destroy the proof of the marriage. Sarah isn't proof of a legal marriage, but she is proof something went on. She's a perfect image of her father."

A bell tinkled slightly in Dorie's head. An image flitted through her mind and was gone. Someone she had seen. Someone she knew.

"Sarah was looking in the window when the two men ransacked the house. She could identify them. That's another reason they might want her dead, although they don't know, at this point, that she saw them. I guess they think she was lost in the woods where they found her mother. They would assume Sarah would starve to death, or that wild animals would get her, or that, if she didn't see anything, it would all blow over. They weren't worried about her at the time."

"Surely . . . surely her father wasn't one of the killers." She held her breath until he answered.

"No. I asked her that. She described the men. Her father wasn't one of them."

She took another sip of coffee. It was cold. She couldn't stand tepid coffee, but she didn't want to reheat it again. "We should tell the people here on the ranch about this—to be watching out for Sarah's safety."

"I thought about that, but they are watching closely for whoever is sneaking around the ranch already. Knowing this part of it won't make it any safer."

"I was sure that whoever was trespassing was after you." Dorie lowered her glance as she turned the cup in her hand. "I've figured out that if someone makes me a widow—if you are murdered or have a so-called accident—that I am fair game again. I'm so worried about you." She looked up at him, and their eyes met. Dorie clinched the cup in her hand. She wanted to throw her arms around him and cry, "Please be safe! Please don't die!" and she realized it wasn't because of her attacker resuming his siege on her, but because she loved Jonah and would fall apart if anything happened to him.

"I've figured that out, too, but tell me, since we are laying all our cards on the table, why does he want you so badly? This doesn't sound like love to me . . . not at all. You mentioned it was all about your land? What's so great about it that he couldn't just go buy some other land somewhere?"

"Oil. That's what's special."

Chapter 19

"Oil? How would he know if there is oil on your land?"

"Because his land abuts mine. I know he's been talking to Navco Oil, and they've done a test well close to the line between our two properties. The way he is after me, not asking me about selling or joining forces, just about marriage, he has a complete takeover in mind. They must have told him something that makes him think there is oil on my land."

"Couldn't you just contact Navco and make a deal with them directly?"

"I could, but I don't think that would change anything. He would still think I'm a sitting duck, just waiting for him to come get me. Whether I drilled or not, it would be all the same to him."

"So when he raped you, he thought that would make you more cooperative? Is that it?"

"Something like that. You see, I'm considered an old maid in this community. I've always been so busy taking care of Big B, both the ranch and the other businesses, that I never had time for men. I'm a wallflower."

"You're far from being a wallflower. You could be the belle of the ball if you put your mind to it. You're beautiful and—"

"Please don't flatter me."

"I'm only telling you the truth."

With his attention on her, she felt her cheeks getting warm and knew that she was blushing.

"When did you take over from your father—running the Big B?"

This subject was easier. She could talk about the ranch or Big B Enterprises at length, but not about herself. "When Bix came back from the war, Father expected him to begin to take the initiative, begin to act like a boss. As I told you, Bix didn't want to run Big B Enterprises or any part of it. That was to have been Danny's, but he didn't make it back from France. Bix began drinking more and more, to escape, I think, from telling Father that he didn't want to do it. I was in the background, watching and learning. When Father gave Bix something to do—a report to fill out, a phone call to make, a deal to broker—it would be me who did it, but I gave Bix all the credit for it. Father didn't know for a long time that Bix wasn't doing anything.

"When Father found out, he threw a fit—screaming and yelling at Bix. I think Father had a stroke then, but he still functioned. Bix took it badly. He was very ashamed of taking credit for the work I had been doing and went on a bender. He was drunk for days. He drove his car off the bridge over the Brazos and drowned. We didn't know if it was accidental or deliberate. When Father found out about it, he had a heart attack. He didn't live long after that.

"I was the only one left, the only one to run Big B. I had to do it. I couldn't let it fail. I had some convincing to do—to the men who worked here who didn't think they could take orders from a woman and to the bankers involved in all the deals and businesses Big B was involved with. When I told them that it was me, not Bix, who had really been running things for the past year, they gave me a chance." She stopped talking, finally out of words.

"And you convinced them," Jonah said.

She nodded her head.

"And you've prospered."

"Yes."

"And now you—we have to keep the enemy at bay so Big B will continue in Barnett hands."

Chapter 20

Jonah expected that revenge, or justice, as he called it, would be sweet, but he was having trouble planning retribution for his sister's death. When he tracked down Letty's location and learned of her murder, he was determined to find her husband and extract satisfaction—although he would never be fully satisfied—for Letty's suffering at the hands of the man who had taken a vow to protect her.

He made a promise to himself to keep Sarah safe at all costs—safe from the man who was her father or from anyone else who might harm her. Whoever the persons were who harmed Letty, they either didn't know about Sarah or must have thought she had been in the woods where her mother died and perished later. If they did any follow-up investigation, they would find out that Jonah came and took his niece away. The logical place for them to look for her would be at her grandparents' home near Waco. Jonah took care to only tell his parents that Sarah was safe. He gave them no clue as to where she, or he, was. They couldn't give away what they didn't know.

When Jonah discovered that Letty's husband lived in Cottonport, he had to create an excuse to linger in that area— an excuse that wouldn't arouse suspicion. The Big B Ranch needed a hand, so he hired on. He never thought he would thank his father for the years he spent "learning the family business." He had spent enough months herding cattle and fixing fences that he felt at home in the job and looked as if that was all he was, a cowboy on a job that was only one in a series of dead-end positions. At the end of the day, he could drive his old rattle-trap truck—the one he had driven since he was a teenager—into town, grab a beer, and play a round of pool or a hand of cards and listen to the conversations going on around him.

It was in that way Jonah found out more about the handsome stranger who had mesmerized his sister and carried her off to her death. He was, indeed, rich. That, at least, hadn't been a lie. He could have afforded to care for Letty in a much better fashion. *So why didn't he?* Jonah wondered. *Maybe his family didn't approve of the marriage? But our family is at least as wealthy and prestigious as his. Maybe it was her disability?*

The most startling thing Jonah learned was that Letty's husband had married again, not after her death, but almost two years prior. His new wife was the daughter of a judge. Except she wasn't really his wife. Letty was his wife at the time of his second marriage.

That means no one knew about his marriage to Letty. That was the reason she had to be eliminated. There would be hell to pay if the judge or his daughter found out about Letty. The second union was bigamous, and any children from that second marriage wouldn't be legal. They would be bastards. He pondered this information and concluded that if anyone found out Sarah was alive she wouldn't be safe. The man couldn't bear the shame of such a discovery, and he might even end up in jail for his shenanigans. Anyone who would kill Letty wouldn't think twice about killing a little girl, even if it was his daughter. Sarah would never be safe until Jonah did something about the whole situation. *What can I do? And how do I prove all this without the marriage license?*

He thought he had Sarah safely hidden away with Mrs. Finch, but that was a tragic mistake. Then Dorie came along with her marriage proposal, and Jonah seized on that as a perfect solution. He could come and go in town without the least suspicion about what he was doing there. As Dorie's husband, he had a place, not only to live, but to fit into the society of Cottonport.

Somewhere along the way, he had gotten wrapped up in Dorie's problem. He had taken her word for it that she had to get married immediately and that it was "business" related. Learning that she was pregnant with another man's baby was a shock. His first thought was that she just didn't want to be saddled with the shame of giving birth to a child out of wedlock, but it was a lot more serious than that. The child wasn't the result of an affair with a married man. It sounded like the man would have, in fact, wanted to marry her, but for the wrong reasons. He was determined to have dominance over Dorie, her land, and her businesses. He was one of those individuals who thought women should have no control over themselves, that everything ought to be delegated to her husband. Jonah had heard enough of men like that, spouting off about "a woman's place." That's not the way it worked with his parents, and it wouldn't be the way it worked with him whenever he got married for real. Dorie wasn't a woman to bow down to a man's rule, and she sure wasn't going to marry someone just because he wanted her to, even if he had raped her to show his superiority. Even if she was pregnant with his child.

So now, here he was, tangled up in Dorie's concerns. He thought this marriage would solve some of his problems, but it had created more. Dorie was so worried about someone trying to make her a widow that she didn't want to let him out of her sight. Personally, he thought she had blown everything out of proportion, and it was about time to tell her so. That evening after supper he would do it—tell her that he didn't think his life was in danger and he had things he needed to be doing. He had his own mysteries to solve, like confirming who Letty's killers were, and who sent them.

After Thanksgiving, everything had returned to the usual schedule. Annie tended to the house, Dorie worked in her office, and Jonah spent his time in the car barn, tinkering with his truck or Crippled Elk's. Sarah followed Annie around the house, asking questions and talking a blue streak. Jonah was glad to see her overcome the morose state she had been in when he first found her. She had put on weight, her chestnut brown hair gleamed red in the sunlight, and her blue eyes sparkled. She smiled often, and he had even heard her laugh.

"It's Monday, Little Bird. Time to gather up the dirty laundry. Go get the sheets off your bed and bring all the clothes you wore this week."

Sarah scampered off to do the chore and returned a few minutes later.

"Here they are, Annie."

"Go take them out to the back porch, Usdi Tsisqua."

When all the clothing and household items had been collected and sorted, the part Sarah thought of as fun began. Annie filled the tub of the much-prized new Maytag electric washer with hot water, drawn from a hose attached to a faucet installed just for that job, then turned on the agitator.

"Annie, can I dump in the soap?" Sarah asked.

"Yes, but let me see how much you are putting in. We don't want too much."

Sarah carefully dipped a cup into the box of Quick Arrow Laundry Flakes and showed it to Annie. "Yes, it is just right. Pour it into the water. Slowly," she said and watched until the soap was dissolved. "It is your job again. Put one piece in at a time."

Sarah dropped a towel or a sheet or a shirt into the swirling water and watched as it became caught up in the back and forth motion and worked its way to the bottom. Clothing came first, while the water was at its cleanest.

Ladies clothing, that is, not the dirty dungarees or overalls. Those would be last.

Annie stirred them with a long, smooth stick as the washer churned the water to and fro. When she had determined they had washed enough, Annie flipped the lever that turned on the wringer that was attached to the back. Sarah stood on a stool and watched as Annie used the stick to push the wet cloth into the turning rollers that squeezed the water out and deposited the steaming cloth into a tub of fresh water on the other side. When Sarah was tempted to use her fingers to aid the process, Annie cautioned, "No! You'll get your fingers in between the rollers, and they will get squashed flat! No use hands. I use stick!"

Annie then went to the rinse side and stirred the items again. When she had determined all the soap was out, she swung the wringer to the side, and once again, the items were run through the wringer. The now-clean laundry was placed into a wicker basket.

This procedure was repeated until all the household's washing was clean. Then it was time to hang it on the clothesline. Sarah liked this part, too. First, she took an item from the wicker basket and handed it to Annie. While Annie was shaking the wrinkles out, Sarah took two clothespins from the cloth bag and was ready to hand them, one at a time, to Annie so she could pin the wash to the clothesline that stretched across the side of the backyard. Annie told her that it was an important job, as it helped to speed up the process. Annie told stories as she hung up the clothes—stories of Cherokee legends that had been told for countless decades and in countless locations as the Native Americans were driven from their homes and forced to find a new sanctuary.

Sarah was handing clothespins and Annie was pinning clothes one day when a buzzing sound became louder, and they looked to the sky to find the source.

"Look, Annie! There's something up there! It's flying! What is it?"

"It is what is called an air-e-o-plane. It is a machine white men have made so they can fly like the birds."

They watched it cross the blue expanse.

"How does it stay up there?"

"I do not know. The men who build them are very smart. They know how to make them do it."

"When you tell me that someday I will fly, is that what you mean?"

"Anything is possible, Little Bird. Someday you may fly in one of those areoplanes, but should it be that you don't fly in a machine, your spirit can soar like the birds even when your body is here on the ground."

Sarah thought about Annie's answer. She didn't understand about soaring spirits, but she determined that one day she would fly in one of those machines.

The clothes had to dry and be gathered in by dark, and there was always the likelihood of rain, in which case Annie and Sarah would have to hurry outside and bring in the wash before it got wet again.

Late in the afternoon, Annie said, "Sarah, get the good basket and the laundry basket and come help." The clothing that needed ironing went in the good basket. The next morning, bright and early, Wooley Cotton was there in his rattling old van, bringing back the freshly ironed clothing his wife had worked over the previous week and picking up the newly washed items needing her attention. Agnes Cotton supported the two of them with her work, and her husband did all the pick-up and delivery.

When Dorie first suggested paying to have the ironing done, Annie had protested. "Miss Dorie, you already pay me plenty. You don't need to pay someone else to do what I been doin' ever since I came to work for you."

"It has been just the two of us, Annie. Now there are two more people in the household, and I have the idea that a man and a child will make a big increase to your workload. Besides, poor Mrs. Cotton has to earn enough to feed the two of them since her husband lost his job."

"It wasn't just the two of us at first. I did the ironing for Mr. Big and Mr. Bix and even a little for poor Mrs. Barnett, and for you. I surely can iron for you and Mr. Jonah and Little Bird."

But Dorie would not be persuaded, so Annie gave in, and Wooley appeared every Tuesday morning to pick up and deliver, and Annie gave him the envelope with bills and coins in it she had set aside. He was always grateful. "Thankee, thankee, Miz Runningdeer. See you next week," he'd say.

The evenings went the same, washday or not. After supper, after the dishes were done, Annie retired to her cottage, and Dorie, Jonah, and Sarah relaxed in the living room. As November gave way to December, days were comfortable, and evenings were chilly. Jonah built a blazing fire, and Sarah settled on the rug in front of it, as usual, constructing an imaginary home from pictures cut out of a catalogue.

"Christmas isn't far off," Dorie commented. "I think Santa Claus is going to have to bring a nice present for all of us to enjoy."

"Oh?" Jonah said. "And what might that be?"

"Santa's presents are always surprises," she replied.

"Mama told me about Santa Claus," Sarah said, a sad look on her face. "But he never came to see us."

Dorie and Jonah looked at each other, each determined to make this a memorable Christmas for the much-loved child. As quickly as the sadness fell upon Sarah, it lifted and she was back to her pretend house. "Look, Uncle Jonah. Look at the washing machine. It's just like the one Annie has on the back porch. See?" Jonah leaned over to look more closely.

Pop! Dorie thought the pop she heard was from the log Jonah had put on the fire only a few minutes before. It wasn't until she saw the spray of glass from the shattered window flying across the room that she comprehended that it wasn't the fire that had made the noise, but a gunshot.

Chapter 21

"You wanted to meet?"

"No! I don't want to track around on the damn riverbank like I'm some fugitive." Grainger held the receiver tightly to his ear and grasped the speaker in his other hand.

"You put the paper in the window."

"So you'd call. I'm not getting back on a damn horse and going to the back of beyond to talk to you. I'll talk from the comfort of my office."

"It's dangerous doing it this way. What if someone is listening, say the operator or someone on the party line?"

"So they listen. We aren't saying anything incriminating. Besides, this isn't a party line, and I hope you have better sense than to use a phone on one."

"All right. Talk."

"You aren't getting any results."

"Things don't always go as planned."

"They'd better start going better."

"Or what? You'll get someone else for the job?"

"I paid you . . . I paid you for this job, and I want results."

"I made an attempt."

"So I heard. It failed."

"The target moved at the last minute. There are variables, you know. I can't make someone stand still so I can . . . do my job."

"You'd better have a plan that works. I want this done and done soon!"

"He's holed up out there . . . hard to get to. I'm going to have to lure him out in the open."

"Then you'd better have a good plan to lure him."

"I do."

"Because if you fail again, I'm going to have to bring someone else in to do the job, and one of the things he'll do is get rid of anyone who could talk. Understand?"

"If you're talking about getting rid of me, you'd better think again. You have more weaknesses than I do. Maybe *I'll* get rid of anyone who could talk. You might be the one to go."

When Grainger replaced the earpiece on the side of the telephone base, his hand shook so badly it took him several tries. Anger that he usually kept bottled spilled over, and he swept the papers from his desk. He picked up first one book, then another, and threw it across the room. Getting to his feet, he kicked his chair so hard it toppled over. His secretary opened the door. "Are you all right, Mr. Grainger?"

"Does it look like I'm all right? Get the hell out!" he yelled.

She closed the door behind her softly. "He can have a heart attack and die, for all I care. I've had enough of these temper tantrums. I'll not check on him ever again!" she said, being careful to say it quietly, so he couldn't hear.

Everyone at the ranch was on edge, from the hands who worked with the cattle and were tasked with looking for trespassers, to the inhabitants of the Big House who lived in fear of another bullet coming through a window. Jonah wanted to tell the sheriff about what had happened, but Dorie insisted that the man who wanted to make her a widow was an important person and might have the sheriff on his payroll. "It might make things worse," she said. "It might give someone an opportunity that he wouldn't have had otherwise." Jonah thought that was a far-fetched idea, that they needn't have fear of a lawman, but he gave in to Dorie's concern.

For all the stress at the Big B Ranch, Christmas was still filled with joy. Sarah was beside herself with excitement. She had been assured that Santa Claus would, indeed, visit her this year.

"Probably he didn't come last year, and the year before, because you lived so far out in the country he couldn't find you," Dorie explained, and Jonah backed up her story.

"I wonder what Santa will bring me?" she said several times a day.

"You're just going to have to wait and see," came the answer from Annie, or Dorie, or Jonah.

Packages from Montgomery Ward and Sears & Roebuck arrived at the mailbox up on the road almost daily, and Crippled Elk brought them to the Big House in his truck. Some of them were whisked away before Sarah could puzzle over them. Jonah placed orders of his own. He tried to be on hand when the old pickup arrived with the mail, taking charge of certain parcels which he immediately took to his room before even Dorie was able to see them.

Crippled Elk cut a cedar tree and attached a wooden base, adjusting it several times so it would stand straight. Dorie ordered Noma lights and glass balls, and one evening a few days before Christmas, they all gathered to decorate the tree. Annie stayed at the Big House to help in the festivities instead of retiring to her cottage as she usually did. This was a big event, not having occurred in many years.

"You know . . . now that I think about it, I believe there is a box of old ornaments you and your brothers used to put on the tree every year," Annie mused.

"Do we still have that?" Dorie paused in hanging a gold ball on a high branch.

"I 'magine it's in the attic," Annie said.

"I forgot to order a star to go on top," Dorie said. "It would be wonderful if I could find that box. I haven't thought about it in years."

"Not since your papa died, I reckon."

"And Bix. Bix died that year, too. I didn't want Christmas after that."

"A star goes on top?" Sarah asked. "Why?"

"It is the symbol of the star that led the Wise Men to the Baby Jesus." Dorie replied.

"The what? Who?" Sarah was puzzled.

"You haven't ever heard the Christmas story?" Dorie asked.

"I don't think so."

"Unequa, the Great Spirit, he sent the Baby Jesus to be born, and he made a bright star shine so that the three Wise Men, they were chiefs of their tribes, would know where to find him," Annie explained. "And they followed where the star told them to go, and they brought presents to show he was a great chief, greater than all the other chiefs."

"The story is in the Bible," Dorie explained.

"I have a Bible!" Sarah was excited. "Mama said it used to belong to Grandma and Grandpa Crandall. Mama said I was just a tiny baby when we lived with them. I don't remember."

"Yes, it was in the drawer when I packed your things, and I put it in the suitcase with your clothes," Jonah put a red glass ball toward the top of the tree. "Do you have it in your room?"

"Yes. I'll go get it." Sarah took off in a run.

"Don't run," Dorie cautioned. "You might slip and fall down the stairs."

"You're beginning to sound like a mother already," Annie commented. "Getting your practice before you have one of your own."

Dorie didn't speak, but the statement set her to thinking. This thing that was such a tragedy might turn out to not be so bad after all. Christmas with a child in the house was an unexpected pleasure.

Sarah soon returned with the large, worn, black book. It only took a few more ornaments and the decorations were complete. "Sarah and I will look in the attic tomorrow and see if we can find the box of old ornaments," Annie said.

They took their usual chairs around the fireplace. Sarah stretched out on the rug before the flames, and Jonah turned to the age-old story and began to read.

Everyone listened raptly as his voice read the account of the first Christmas, of stars and angels and visiting kings. By the time he finished, Sarah was fast asleep.

"I thought this was going to be a somber time," Dorie said, "what with keeping the curtains and drapes so tightly closed that the sunlight can't even find its way in."

"And not being able to go outside, not at all." Jonah added the restriction that bothered him most.

"But it is not somber," Annie said. "It is joyous, as the birth of Unequa's son ought to be."

Chapter 22

At Big B Ranch, the Christmas tree had been taken down, and the ornaments, both new and old, had been stored away in boxes in the attic. Dorie pushed away the thoughts that buzzed around in her head as she worked. *Jonah and Sarah won't be here next Christmas. She won't see this ornament that is her favorite. I won't see the light on her face as she comes down the steps and sees the presents under the tree. I won't have Jonah standing beside me as we watch her wonder at the splendor of the toys she receives. Next year, it will just be me and Annie . . . and the baby, of course.* She refused to think about what it would be like in a year. She refused to think about how life would be without them.

"A little house!" Sarah exclaimed on Christmas morning. "Santa brought me a little house!"

"It's called a dollhouse," Dorie explained. Sarah alternated between moving the tiny furniture from room to room and playing with the doll she had received.

"See, Sarah. She has long blond curls, like your mother used to have," Jonah said. He was torn between wanting Sarah to always remember her mother and wanting her to forget the terrible time she had living in the house in the woods, hungry and frightened.

Each evening they sat in the living room, as was the established habit, but instead of reading, they listened to the Christmas present Dorie had given them all: a radio. After supper, after the dishes were done—because no one would think about leaving Annie in the kitchen washing dishes alone—they all settled in front of the set and listened to music or tales of adventure or laughed at the antics of the comedians. Jonah would carefully turn the dial until the voices coming from the magnificent piece of furniture were as clear as he could get them. After they became familiar with the programs, they each had their favorites and would take turns choosing what to listen to. Annie favored music, especially the Carnation Contented Hour. Dorie liked the music, too, and the Charlie Chan mysteries. Her favorite, though, the one she didn't want to miss, was when Eleanor Roosevelt spoke about women's issues. Jonah preferred Bring 'Em Back Alive, and he liked all the comedians—Jack Benny, Burns and Allen, and Fred Allen—and he liked to listen to Franklin Roosevelt, who spoke weekly. Sarah liked The Adventures of Captain Diamond and Buck Rogers in the 25th Century. She loved the ideas of things that were yet to be invented.

Although there were programs on the radio during the daytime, they spent their days in work, each in their own area. Dorie stayed in her office, keeping books on the various businesses that made up Barnett Enterprises. Jonah, having become bored with staying in the house, gradually became involved. He had asked enough questions that Dorie, seeing that he was truly interested, started showing him the records. When she began, she was surprised when he not only understood what she was talking about, but suggested other systems of keeping books—methods that were better than the way she had been doing it. Together, they went through the ledgers and files and organized everything in a way that made it easier for her to find what she was looking for and have facts and figures at her fingertips.

"How do you know all this?" she asked him.

"My father has his hands in a lot of pies," he said, "and he insisted that my brother, Thomas, and I learn them, too."

Sarah was learning things, also. She helped with all the housework and especially enjoyed laundry day. If it didn't rain, Monday was washing day, followed by the day Wooley Cotton brought the ironing back and picked up the basketful his wife would send back the following week.

One Tuesday, just as the year was turning from winter into spring, the old panel-van pulled into the yard, but it wasn't Wooley who came to the house bearing hangers of clothing and a pile of folded items.

"Where's Wooley?" Annie asked, suspicion making her frown.

"Remember that icy spell we had the other day?" asked the man who was wrapped up in layers of scarves pulled high around his lower face and a knit cap pulled down over his forehead. All that showed were his eyes. "Well, Uncle Wooley, he slipped and fell, and we think his ankle is broke. He can't stand on it. He asked me to deliver for him." His eyes scanned the yard and doorway. "You wanna take these? Or should I bring them in the house for you? I got more in the truck."

"I'll take them," Annie said. Sarah hung back and said nothing.

He brought the second load, received the envelope with Mrs. Cotton's money in it and, with a brief "Thank you," started toward the truck. "I'll see you next week, if Uncle Wooley isn't any better," he said.

"You better not forget what you came for," Annie reminded him. "Sarah, get the basket of ironing." Sarah sat it down next to the step as he returned.

Time went by, and a spot of daffodils bloomed at the corner of the house, but winter held its ground. It rained on Monday. Tuesday, however, was clear and warm, so Annie and Sarah did a large amount of washing. Wednesday morning dawned cloudy and cold. "It wouldn't surprise me if we didn't get some snow out of this next weather," Jonah said at the breakfast table. "Flowers or not, it's still February."

Dorie had been up early and dressed in her overalls for a visit to the barn to talk to Burt. "No sense putting on a dress on a day like this," she said. "I'll be warmer in long-johns, overalls, and flannel."

"You're pretty no matter what you wear," Jonah had replied.

Her head told her not to believe him, but her heart sang at the words.

Don't listen to him. He's just flattering you. He doesn't mean it.

When she returned from the barn, she went into her office, where Jonah had been working.

I don't know what he thinks he could gain by flattering me. Things are what they are. They aren't going to change if I listen to his compliments.

"I've pulled the records from the past several years. Let's go over them and see if we can come up with a plan for 1933," Jonah said.

"You mean, if *I* can come up with a plan." She knew she sounded testy.

His eyebrows raised, as if to say, "What happened to you?" but he replied, "That's what I meant to say." He spread the ledger sheets before her.

Annie and Sarah were in the kitchen, mixing batter for cookies when the familiar truck pulled up near the back door, leaving the motor running. A bundled figure descended the running board, arms full.

"Old Wooley not getting any better?" Annie asked. "This is a month he's been laid up."

"We reckon it might a' been broke. He's a bit better, though. Wouldn't be surprised if he's not back on the route next week, if he keeps on like this." He looked up at the sky. "We mighten get some snow tonight."

Annie handed him the envelope. "Thanks. I've got one more handful. Kid, why don't you come to the truck and let me hand it to you? Save me a trip back to the door."

Sarah followed him to the van. When he went in, he turned toward the back. "Let me see. Here it is. Come here and let me hand it to you." Cautiously, taking one small step at a time, she entered the vehicle. She saw the bundle of folded linens across his arms and drew closer, arms outstretched to take them. Suddenly he threw the sheets to the floor and in his hand was a wadded up rag. He grabbed her with his other hand and covered her mouth and nose with the rag. It was the last thing she remembered.

Chapter 23

"Help! Help! He done took her. He took Sarah!"

"Who? Who took Sarah?" Jonah and Dorie jumped to their feet.

"That man who delivers the ironing."

"Wooley? Wooley Cotton took Sarah?" Dorie couldn't wrap her head around that.

"Wooley has a broke ankle. His nephew's been picking up and delivering lately. He got her to come into the truck, and then he just took off with her."

"Stay here," Dorie yelled to Jonah as she raced to the back door. "He's trying to lure you outside where he can get to you." She headed toward the car barn, where Jonah's truck was sitting outside the big double doors. She jumped in it and took off at her usual speed—fast. She never slowed down when she exited the dirt road that led away from the Big House, hitting the county road with her foot to the floorboard. She wished she had taken the time to get her roadster out of the barn. It would have gone a great deal faster, but she had to deal with what she was driving. It was too late now to wish for something different. A couple of miles down the road, she saw the van ahead of her. The driver left the main road and took a narrow dirt road that paralleled the river.

As she grew closer, she noticed that another truck had pulled onto the road and was right behind her. *Good! Someone else is here to help rescue Sarah!* It sped up until it was right on her bumper, then it was bumping her vehicle, hard.

She fought to keep control. She leaned over the steering wheel, using her entire upper body to hold the truck on the road. *Bump!* The other truck drew to the side and rammed her vehicle in the driver's door. It pulled back and rammed again. And again. The steering wheel twisted from her hands, and her vehicle left the road. Hitting a deep ditch on the right-hand side, it tipped. Dorie grabbed the wheel and tried turning back toward the road, but it was too late. The balance had shifted, and suddenly she was rolling over and over, down the steep bank, tossing from the seat to the ceiling and back again, until she came to rest in the Brazos.

Chapter 24

Jonah was only steps behind Dorie when she left the house. There was no way he was going to stay put when Sarah was in danger. When his wife jumped into his truck and took off, he went to the barn for a vehicle. There were two choices: the ranch truck that Dorie usually drove around the home place and her Auburn Speedster. He didn't think twice. He jumped into the Auburn and took off in pursuit.

By the time Jonah reached the paved road, he had it up to sixty miles an hour—faster than he had ever driven in his life. The Speedster had more power, but he wasn't sure he could handle it at any greater speed. It only took a few minutes to have the vehicles ahead of him in sight, and he saw them make the turn onto the river road. He expected to see Dorie ahead of him, but he didn't expect to see another truck pull out from behind some bushes, speed up until it was right on her tail, and start ramming her—first the back bumper then, when she slowed to gain control of the swerving truck, give a mighty shove from the driver's side. With horror, Jonah watched his truck roll over and over, with Dorie's body being tossed about like a bale of hay being destroyed by a mad bull, until at last it came to rest in the Brazos. The driver of the truck that had rammed her paused momentarily to look at the results of his attack then sped off.

Follow the truck way ahead in the distance that has Sarah? Or stay and see to Dorie? His head took him both ways, but Dorie was in immediate danger. He didn't know about Sarah but hoped that whatever scheme was afoot didn't include harming the child immediately.

Throwing on the brakes, he slid to the side of the dirt road and jumped out, running and falling down the steep embankment until he reached the mangled truck, which lay upside down, half-in and half-out of the Brazos.

"Dorie! Sweetheart! Hold on! I'll get you out." He reached in through the broken window of the driver's side door and felt her arm. She stirred slightly. *She's still alive. Thank you, God! She's still alive!*

Blood covered her body and soaked her clothing. It didn't look critical, though, more like the glass had made hundreds of tiny cuts in her skin.

"Mister Jonah!" He heard Crippled Elk call to him from the road. "Miss Dorie, is she . . . is she?"

"She's alive, but I need help getting her out of the truck."

It took several minutes for the man to make his way down, his disability causing him to take each step with stumbling slowness. When he reached where Jonah sat on the ground trying to cradle Dorie's head with his arm through the window, he surveyed the situation then said, "Mister Jonah, if you get ahold of the door right here"—he indicated a spot—"I'll get this side. I think we can get it open a bit, maybe far enough to get her out."

"We have to hurry," Jonah said. "That willow tree is holding the truck back. If it gives, the truck will wash on out into the deep water and sink."

It took several tries. The door moved an inch each time, but at last they had it open enough that Jonah could slip his hands and arms underneath Dorie and pull her out as if she were lying on a board. He thought of trying to find or make a real board to work under her but decided it would take too long. Time was of the utmost importance at this point. He had to get her to a doctor.

"Crippled Elk, which is closest—the doctor's office or home?"

"Home is a lot closer. Besides, if Doc is out making house calls, which is what he does of a morning, there wouldn't be anyone at his clinic. Annie, she'd be the best one to know what to do."

Gathering the limp body into his arms, Jonah slowly made his way back up the bank. Dorie moaned and stirred in his arms. "Shh . . . I've got you. We're going home." They reached the top, and he lifted her over the door and into the passenger seat. "I know this isn't going to be comfortable, Sweetheart, but hold on. We'll be home soon."

Dorie lifted her head and looked around, dazed. "Sarah . . . where is Sarah?"

"Sarah is safe. Don't worry about her." He hoped he wasn't lying when he spoke the words, but he had to tend to what was right in front of him. By now, the van with Sarah in it was long gone. He'd put his mind on that problem as soon as he got Dorie home in bed with Annie watching over her.

He drove home as fast as he dared without jostling her too much. He yelled for Annie as soon as he climbed out of the Speedster. "Get her bed ready for her," he said. "Hurry!" He climbed the stairs behind the woman who was muttering what sounded like prayers in her native tongue and carefully placed Dorie on the pristine bed.

"Oh, it hurts," she said, her voice stronger than before.

"Don't you worry. Annie is here. I'll take care of you good." Annie started removing the bulky coat that had kept most of the flying glass from doing more damage. "You know I always take good care of you."

"I know, Annie. I know you do." Dorie tried to sit up and assist with undressing, but she moaned and fell back against the pillows.

"Shh, now, shh. Let Annie do it for you." She drew the boots from Dorie's feet and started on the overalls. "Mister Jonah, you help me ease these off her." They worked together to get the heavy clothes removed. The flannel shirt came next, then the long johns.

"I don't see any big wounds," Jonah said. "The blood is coming from lots of little cuts on her face and hands."

"That's a good thing, but that don't tell us whether she has anything broke, or if anything inside is messed up."

Jonah ran his hands over Dorie's arms then her legs. "They seem smooth and unbroken, but I can't tell much. Let's get the blood washed off."

"I'll fix some water . . .," Annie said and left the room. Only a minute later she returned from the hall bath with a metal dishpan. She went into Dorie's bathroom and filled it with warm water. When she approached the bed, Jonah took it and the washcloth from her.

"I'll do this. You go call the doctor. Tell him to come as quickly as he can."

"Yessir. I will," Annie said and hurried from the room.

Jonah took the warm, wet cloth and ran it over Dorie's arms and hands. The arms were devoid of cuts, but rivulets of blood had run under the shirtsleeves and made red paths on her pale skin. On the back of one hand, a deeper laceration still oozed. *That will need a bandage.* He continued gently wiping, checking every inch for any pieces of glass that might still be imbedded in her flesh.

He moved on to her face. She roused as the warm cloth touched her cheek. Opening her eyes, she looked deeply into his eyes. "What happened to me?"

"You were pushed off the road by someone in a black pickup. You rolled over and over and ended up in the Brazos. Crippled Elk and I came along and found you. We got you out, and here you are in your own bed."

"Sarah! Where's Sarah?" She tried to sit up but moaned and fell back.

He put his hands on her shoulders to hold her to the pillow. "Be still. We still don't know how badly you are hurt."

"But . . . Sarah?"

"The man who took her got away with her." His heart lurched as he said it.

Dorie didn't speak for a minute. "I'm sore. My head hurts. But I don't think anything is broken." She moved, first her toes, then her legs. "They hurt, but like they are bruised." She wriggled her fingers and lifted her arms. "See, they're not broken." She turned her head from side to side. "I'll be plenty bruised, but I'm OK." She looked at Jonah. "You have to go find Sarah. But be careful. They weren't after Sarah. They were after you."

"I know."

"You know?"

"Yes. I figured it out. They thought I was in the truck. They thought they were killing me."

"Yes."

"If they were after Sarah, they wouldn't have bothered to push my truck into the river. If it was her they were after, they'd have just gone on with her."

She turned her head and stared at the wall. After a minute, she said, "How did you get to me so fast?"

He grinned. "I drove your Speedster."

She managed a small smile. "That's some car, isn't it?" Suddenly, her expression turned into a grimace, and she put her hands on her stomach. Jonah looked at her body under the sheet and saw the tightening muscles. "Ahhh . . . something's happening with the baby," she said in a panicked voice.

Chapter 25

Annie appeared at the doorway. "Mister Jonah, the doctor is on his way, but you'd better come talk on this telephone call."

"What does he want to talk to me for? He just needs to get here, fast. I think the baby is coming."

"It's not the doctor who wants to talk to you. It's Wooley Cotton."

"He has Sarah! He took her!"

"No. Not him. The phone rang just as I hung up from the doctor, and it was Wooley. You go let him tell you. He can explain."

Jonah bounded down the stairs to pick up the telephone in the office. "Where's my niece?" he demanded. "She'd better not be hurt, or so help me God, I'll kill you!"

"Mr. Crandall, it wasn't me what took her. I swear. This man came to my house 'bout a month ago. He had a gun. He said he would kill me and my wife if I told anyone. He said he'd watch my house and know. Every Tuesday he'd show up and take my truck to make the delivery to your wife's house. He'd take the ironed clothes and bring back more. He even gave me the money Annie sent with him, plus a little 'for bein' quiet about it,' he said. That first time, there was another man what stayed with us. He had a gun, too. When the first man came back, they both left . . . said they'd be back. After that first time, it were just the one man what came—the one who took the van and did the delivery.

"Mr. Crandall, after that first time, after I got the money due my wife plus some, and nothin' bad happened, well, we decided just to go along with it. Why not? We couldn't see no harm. Besides, he said he'd know if we told and come back to kill us. So we kept our mouths shut."

"Where is Sarah? That's what I want to know. What did he do with Sarah?"

"That's what I'm fixin' to tell you. When he came back this mornin' and handed my wife her money, he says, 'I won't be back no more.' I goes out to the truck to get the basket of ironing, like usual, and there was your little girl, Sarah, sound asleep. I got her here at my house. She's fine and good. She was right scared when she first woke up, but she knows me and knows I wouldn't hurt her for the world."

"Let me talk to her."

"Well, sir. I can't do that. We don't have no telephone at our house. I had to come down here to my neighbor's house to call you. You come on to my house and get her. My wife's watchin' over her."

Wooley paused before continuing. "I sure am shamed by whatever went on, Mr. Crandall. I wisht I had been able to stand up to that fellow what took her. I surely didn't know what he was planning on doin'. I don't know what he meant by taking the child."

Jonah got directions to the Cotton home, then went back upstairs to Dorie's room.

"Sarah's safe," he told Dorie and Annie. "Wooley Cotton's wife is taking care of her. Wooley said some man forced them to let him use his van to deliver the ironing here every week. He was just waiting for the chance to snatch Sarah, knowing I would follow. It was a setup to get me out where they could kill me."

"Thank the Great Spirit she is safe," Annie said. "You are going after her?"

"Yes."

Dorie moaned. "No . . ."

"They think they took care of me," he said to Dorie. "They think I'm dead. I'll be safe until they find out differently."

Dorie moaned again. He started to speak, but Annie interrupted him.

"You go get Little Bird. We're gonna have us a baby here."

"Isn't it too early?" He wished he hadn't said that aloud. He knew the answer without asking. He only hoped that Dorie would survive, that the accident that was causing early labor hadn't done something life-threatening. A lot of women died in childbirth without having gone through something like Dorie had. He didn't want to leave his wife, but he had to get Sarah and reassure her she was safe. *I've been telling her I would keep her safe, but I didn't do a very good job.*

Chapter 26

It was complicated following Wooley's directions along the country roads to find his home. When Jonah finally pulled up in front of the neat little house, a dog barked at him, and Wooley walked out onto the front porch.

"Mr. Crandall?" the old man asked as Jonah stepped out of the Speedster.

"That's me. Where's Sarah?" He strode to the steps and cleared them in one step.

"She's in here." Wooley opened the front door and ushered Jonah in. "Go on through to the kitchen."

"Here's your uncle," the thin woman sitting at the white wood table said, and Sarah looked up.

"Uncle Jonah!" She jumped up and lifted her arms to be picked up. She looked happy to see him, but she didn't look injured in any way, nor did she appear to have been crying. "A bad man carried me off, Uncle Jonah. When I got into the van to get the ironing, he held a cloth over my nose, and I went to sleep."

"We figure it was chloroform," Mrs. Cotton said.

"When I woke up, Mr. Wooley was getting me out of the truck, and we were at his house. I didn't even know when we left home."

"I found her when I went to get this week's ironing. It's a good thing I went out there as soon as that feller brought the van back, or else she might have woke up alone and been scared."

"When I woke up, I *was* scared, because I didn't know where I was, but Mister Wooley told me I was at his house, and Mrs. Wooley was here, and everything was OK." She paused and looked down. "Well, I was sick just a little, but I feel better now."

Jonah looked at Mrs. Cotton. "She threw up a little, but I gave her some sips of water, and she got to feeling better."

"Like I said, I sure am sorry to be mixed up in this business. I had no idea what was going to happen," the old man said. "Taking a child, that's somethin' plum outrageous."

"Mr. and Mrs. Cotton, I understand that you were forced to go along with the man, or men, but let me ask you this. Could you identify either of them if you saw them again?"

The couple looked at each other, and Jonah saw the husband shake his head slightly. "I don't rightly know. I don't know if I 'member their faces well enough to identify them." Jonah knew that their fear of the pair of gunmen would keep them silenced.

"I thank you for rescuing Sarah. I need to take her home now." He turned and started back through the house.

Mrs. Cotton rose and followed him. "Do you still want me to do your ironing every week? I'd understand it if you didn't. It was a terrible thing that happened."

"I'll leave that decision to my wife and Annie. Go ahead as usual this week, and Annie will let you know." He turned and faced the pair. "But if anything like this comes up again, you must let someone know. If you had done it this time, Sarah would never have been taken."

When Sarah saw what car her uncle had driven, she said, "Did Miss Dorie let you borrow her car?"

"Well, Punkin, she didn't know that I borrowed it."

"Oh . . . you are going to be in a lot of trouble when she finds out!"

"Yes?" he spat into the phone.

"It's done."

"Are you sure?"

"His truck is upside down in the Brazos. I put it there. I saw it go off the road. Is that sure enough?"

"Have you seen the body?"

"No."

"When I see the body, I'll pay you." He hung up.

Chapter 27

Jonah mulled over how much to tell Sarah about the car chase and wreck. Finally, he said, "Dorie went chasing after the man who took you. She was driving my truck, and she had a wreck, so I had to drive something else. She didn't mind, I don't think, that I drove her car. I'm taking good care of it."

"And she didn't take good care of your truck?"

He smiled. "I guess you can say that. I'll need to get myself another vehicle."

"Did Miss Dorie get hurt?"

"Yes. The doctor is on his way to check her over, but I don't think anything is broken."

"Except your truck?"

"Except my truck. But she'll be in bed for a while, until she gets to feeling better."

Sarah accepted that and sat quietly for a mile or so. Then she said, "I think maybe the man who was pretending to be Mr. Wooley's nephew was one of the men who was in our house, Mama's and mine, the day she went into the woods and didn't come back."

Jonah was amazed. He looked over at Sarah, where she sat staring at the dashboard, a slight frown on her face. "It was the same man?" He couldn't fathom a connection.

"Maybe," she said. "His voice sounded the same."

"You heard him speak when he was in your house?"

"Yes. They were looking for something, and they said, 'It's not here' and 'I can't find it anywhere.'"

"So Mr. Cotton's nephew sounded like one of them?"

Her forehead wrinkled in thought. "Yes. I think so." Her face cleared. "It's fun riding in Miss Dorie's automobile. Why don't you get one like this, since your truck is smashed?"

"You'd like that, huh?"

"Yes!"

As they drove home, Jonah thought about Sarah's statement about the identity of her kidnapper, but he decided she must be mistaken. *What connection could there be between Lonnie Grainger having Letty killed and some man wanting to marry Dorie and take over her land? Probably they just sound similar. Both have a low voice, or a high one, or maybe an accent.*

When they reached the Big House, the doctor's Model A Ford was parked by the front steps. Jonah pulled Dorie's car around to the back, and he and Sarah went in through the kitchen.

"Let's go upstairs. I'll see how Dorie is doing and what the doctor says," Jonah said. "You go play in your room until I see if she feels like seeing you." He felt sure Dorie was going to want to see Sarah, to be sure she was home and in good shape, but he wanted to speak with the doctor without the presence of the child.

The man coming out of Dorie's bedroom was short and pudgy, balding, and wearing gold-rimmed glasses. "Doctor?" Jonah called to him as he approached. "I'm Dorie's husband. How is she doing? What can you tell me?"

"Mr. Crandall," the doctor adjusted his glasses and looked up at Jonah. "She has no broken bones, and the cuts she received are minor, but I'm afraid she is in labor. If it continues, she will deliver the baby in the next few hours, which is far too soon. We'll just have to wait and see if it can survive."

"My wife, though, will she be all right?"

"Again, we'll have to wait and see. Ordinarily, I would say yes. She's young and healthy, and there is no reason she wouldn't have a normal, uneventful birth, but having been through such a bad wreck and the baby coming so early, well . . . as I said, we'll have to wait and see."

"If there is anything, anything at all you can do . . ." Jonah ran out of words.

"Now, son"—the doctor patted Jonah on the arm—"I know. I know you love your wife, and your baby, too. I'll do everything I can to save both of them." He started toward the stairs. Pausing, he said, "I'm going to my office now. There is nothing I can do here at the moment that Annie can't do just as well. Either the labor will progress, or it will stop. Let's hope it stops. The baby needs to stay where it is for another month or more at the least. I'll be back after office hours, unless you need me before then."

He left, and Jonah went to the bedroom door. Opening it a crack, he peeped in before entering. Seeing Dorie propped up on the pillows with Annie sitting at her side, he went to her bedside. "Hi there. Feeling any better?"

"Some. I'm awfully sore, and I know it'll be worse before it gets better. Did you get Sarah?"

"Yes. Do you feel like seeing her?"

"Oh, yes. Is she all right? Was she hurt? I'll bet she is terrified."

"I'll let you see for yourself." He went down the hall to Sarah's room, where she was lying across her bed, adjusting her doll's dress. "Do you want to see Dorie?" he asked.

"Yes!" Sarah said and bounced off the bed. She followed him down the hall and into Dorie's room. "Hi!" she said and leaned against the bed at Dorie's side. She reached out and patted Dorie's hand. "I'm sorry you got hurt." She gently kissed a place that was beginning to turn an ugly purple. "That's what my mama used to do when I got hurt. She kissed it to make it better."

"Oh, Sarah, honey. I'm sure your kisses will make me get better in a hurry." Tears came to her eyes as she squeezed the small hand that held hers so carefully. "We were so worried about you. Are you OK?"

"Yes. That bad man put a rag over my nose, and it made me go to sleep. When I woke up, Mr. Wooley Cotton was there, and we were at his house. I don't remember going there. I was a little sick when I woke up, but Mrs. Wooley gave me some water, and Mr. Wooley gave me a peppermint, and I'm all better now." She studied Dorie. "Are you going to get all better?"

"Yes, I am. I'm going to get all better like you," Dorie said convincingly.

"I think that now that Mr. Jonah and Little Bird are here, I'm going to go down to the kitchen and fix us something to eat. It's past dinnertime. Are you hungry?" Annie asked Sarah.

"Yes. Mrs. Cotton asked me if I wanted something to eat, but I was still kinda sick and said no, thank you, but I'm kind of hungry now."

"I'm glad you remembered your manners," Dorie said. "Run along, now, and get something to eat."

"I'll be along directly," Jonah said. "I'll stay with Dorie for a few minutes."

When Annie and Sarah left, he said, "You see? She seems fine. I guess she was sound asleep during the scary part, that is, when they were on the road. She went to sleep, then she woke up, and although she was in a different place, nothing really happened that scared her, other than having a cloth put over her nose."

"That would be frightening to me. I'm glad she's taking it so well. With everything that has happened to her, I thought she would be traumatized." As she spoke, her voice got tighter, and she put both hands on her belly.

Jonah put one hand beside hers and felt the muscles tightening into a hard knot. "Does it hurt when it does that?" he asked.

Dorie grimaced, shutting her eyes and clinching her teeth. Finally, she took a breath. "Yes, it does, but not real bad. Doctor Powell said if I stay very still, they may stop. I hope they do. It's too early for the baby to come."

"I know it is, but I have no idea how early. We haven't talked about that."

"About six weeks early." She stared off, lost in thought. "Or, to make people believe it is your baby, about nine or ten weeks early. Much, much too early."

She was lost in thought. Finally, she said, "It was no accident. It was deliberate."

"I know. Whoever did it thought it was me they were killing. You were in my truck and dressed in men's clothing. From a distance it would seem like a man was driving." He took the chair that Annie had vacated. "I don't know that I believed you, at first, but I do now. Someone is determined to do away with me."

"Yes." Tears came to her eyes. "You have to be careful. You have to accept that."

"I believe you, Dorie, but think about this: it might not have to do with you. It might have to do with Letty and Sarah."

"Letty and Sarah?" She turned her head toward him. "Why would someone be after you because of them?"

"Because I want to expose Letty's husband as a murderer and bigamist."

"But if it had to do with them, wouldn't they have harmed Sarah while they had her? Instead, they returned her, safe and sound."

Jonah dropped his head. "I guess you're right," he finally admitted.

"He wants to make me a widow. A pregnant widow who needs a man to get by. A pregnant widow who accepts a rapist as my savior." She shook her head against the pillow. "Never."

Annie appeared in the doorway. "I brought you a cup of soup. You need a little nourishment to build up your strength. See if you can eat a bit." She set a tray on the side of the bed. "Mr. Jonah, go on down and eat with Little Bird. You need to keep yourself up, too. I have a feeling we all gonna need to be strong these days."

She settled herself beside the bed. "Here, let me spoon you up some of this good bean soup." She held a dishcloth under Dorie's chin as she fed her some of the warm food. Dorie ate half a dozen bites before her head fell back against the pillow.

"That's enough, Annie. Let me rest a minute, then I'll try to do it myself."

"Don't you overdo, now."

"I won't." She closed her eyes and was silent. When she spoke, she said, "Do you remember the time Bix and Dannie said girls couldn't break horses and I was determined to prove them wrong?"

Annie chuckled. "I remember."

"So I got on Bullet, and I held on for dear life. He was working to get me off, and I was working to stay on. He won, but not before everyone around the place came to watch me."

"Unequa was with you that day. He spared your life."

"How I hurt after that day is how I hurt now. I'm sore all over."

"Unequa was with you today, too. You landed in the Brazos de Dios—the arms of God."

Chapter 28

After she ate the soup Annie brought to her, Dorie drifted off to sleep. Although the baby kicked and moved, there were no more contractions that afternoon. She awoke two hours later and had Annie help her to the bathroom. Annie wanted to go to the attic and find the bedpan stored away from when Dorie's mother was bedridden, but Dorie refused.

"No way am I going to use that thing as long as I can get up," she told Annie. She moaned and groaned as she leaned against the stout woman. "Don't worry, Annie," she said. "It's just aches and pains, not contractions."

Back in bed, she eased against the pillows once again. Jonah stuck his head in the door, and seeing that she was awake asked, "May I come in?"

"Certainly. Come in and visit with me." She smoothed the covers over her bulging belly.

"Are you still having labor pains?"

"No. Not for a couple of hours."

"That's good."

"Yes. Doctor Porter said they might quit, and it looks like they have."

Sarah stuck her head in the door. "Can I come in?"

"Yes. You can. Do you mean 'may I'?"

"Yes, I meant 'may I come in.'"

"Yes, you may. Come visit with me. What have you been doing?"

"I played with my dollhouse for a while, then I colored in my coloring book."

Just then, Dorie's face tensed, and her forehead wrinkled. She put her hands on her belly as she had before. Jonah placed his hand over hers and felt the tightening of the muscles. "They've started again?"

She nodded. "Maybe they'll stop, like before."

Annie came to the door. "I sliced some cookies from the roll I have in the refrigerator. Anyone here want some fresh-baked pecan cookies?"

"Me!" Sarah hopped up and down. "I do. I want some cookies."

"They're the ones you helped me mix up and make into rolls. I'll come pour you a glass of milk to have with them."

"Annie, I'll go pour the milk. You stay here with Dorie," Jonah said.

"Yes. I will do," Annie said. As she walked toward the bed, her face lost its smile, and she studied Dorie. Seeing the expression on her face, she placed her hand on Dorie's belly. When she felt the easing contraction, she nodded once and took a seat in the chair by the bedside. "They have started again?"

"This was the first one in hours," Dorie answered. She looked at the china clock sitting on top of her bureau.

"The doctor, he say to time them," Annie said. "He be back late this afternoon, anyway, but if pains get two to three minutes apart, call him and he will come quick."

There wasn't another contraction for several hours. Doctor Porter came and went, leaving the same instructions: remain in bed, stay quiet, and call him if the pains resumed and stayed and were close together in time.

The contractions began again in earnest in the early hours of the morning. Annie and Jonah took turns sitting with Dorie, who slept until she was awakened by the tightening of the muscles in her abdomen. Jonah was asleep in the overstuffed armchair when she awoke him.

"I think it's happening this time. The contractions are pretty regular at five minutes apart. They're stronger and don't seem to be going away like before. Maybe you'd better go fetch Annie."

When Annie came, she placed her hand on Dorie's belly during one of the labor pains. "Yes. I think this is for real. Mister Jonah, you go call doctor, please. Tell him Miss Dorie is having baby for sure. Tell him come."

When Doctor Porter arrived, the pains were two minutes apart. It was only a short time before the diminutive infant was born.

"It's a girl, tiny but perfect," he told Dorie.

When the newborn was cleaned, Annie folded a diaper as small as she could get it, but it still swallowed the baby. She wrapped her in the white flannel blanket she had laid out earlier and handed her to Dorie. "She is perfect," Annie said as she tucked the child into the crook of Dorie's arm.

"I'll be going now," Doctor Porter said. "Dorie, you rest. Eat and drink plenty, and you'll be as good as new in no time. Don't you try getting up and wearing yourself out."

"What about the baby?" she asked.

"Well, Dorie, it's like I told you before. That wreck brought her long before she should have come. Keep her warm. That's important. Try to get her to nurse as much as possible. That's about it." He rolled down his sleeves and reached for his coat. "I hear they are working on a new device—they call it an incubator—they put premature babies in. It's supposed to help them breathe easier. There's not one in Texas that I know about. Sure not one in Cottonport."

He closed his bag and picked it up. As he opened the bedroom door, he looked back. "I'll come by this evening and check on you." He turned and walked out the door.

Dorie looked at the baby in her arms. Unlike any baby she had ever seen, her skin was almost translucent. Running one finger over the tiny hand, she marveled at the fingers, no larger than a tendril on a vine, and there were no fingernails. Eyes closely shut, there were no eyelashes, either, nor eyebrows. Dorie drew an imaginary brow with her finger. "Edoda not finish her yet. She will grow those later," Annie said.

"I fought loving her," Dorie said, "because of what happened. But . . . but . . ." Tears rolled down her cheeks. "She needs me. She needs my love."

"She will have your love, no matter what Edoda rules."

Dorie glanced up at her friend. "You think she will not live?"

Annie shrugged. "I cannot say what Great Spirit will do."

"But you don't think she'll make it," Dorie pressed.

"She is awfully small to make it. Might have many problems."

Dorie held the bundle closely.

"You want me to call Mister Jonah and Little Bird to see?"

"Yes, do that."

When they entered the room, Sarah held back for a moment, suddenly shy.

"Come closer. You can see her," Dorie urged. Both Jonah and Sarah peeked into the swaddle of blankets to see the slight figure.

"What's her name?" Sarah asked.

"You know, I haven't given any thought about a name." She stared out the window at the pink sky. "She was born just as dawn was breaking. I think Dawn would be a good name for her, to remember how she looks, only a few minutes after her birth."

"That's a good name," Sarah agreed. "Can I hold her?"

Dorie paused. Dawn was so small, and Sarah wasn't used to holding a baby, but if this were the only chance . . . . Dorie fought back her tears. "Yes. Of course you can hold her. Jonah, why don't you sit in the big chair and let Sarah sit beside you." They settled themselves into the cushiony depths. Annie took the baby from Dorie and placed her in Sarah's arms.

"Ooh. She's so little," Sarah said. The blanket had dropped back from the baby's head, exposing her tuft of hair. Sarah ran one finger over it, smoothing it down. "And her hair is the same color as mine." She looked up at Dorie. "Are we going to be sisters?"

The question took Jonah by surprise. *Sisters. They weren't, were they? No, it wasn't possible . . . or was it?*

Chapter 29

Too weak to even nurse, Dawn stopped moving her arms and legs and lay quietly in Dorie's arms. Her mother wouldn't allow her to be placed in the bassinet that had been ordered out of a catalogue. "I'll hold her as long as I can," she said, when it became obvious the child was becoming weaker. Jonah sat beside her, his troubling thoughts whirling in his brain. *Surely not* kept repeating itself, harsh and discordant as a crow in a tree, demanding that people hear its raucous call. *Surely not his baby. Surely not Sarah's sister. Surely not . . .*

Some manner of reasoning inserted itself in his thoughts. *The man who did this, who made this baby, wants Dorie to marry him so he can control her land and assets. Sarah's father is already married. It couldn't be him. It couldn't be him.* Those words replaced the earlier refrain. *It couldn't be him.*

As the room grew dark, Jonah got up to turn on the little lamp on the dressing table and heard Dorie's sobs. The light illuminated far enough that he could see her drop her head and gently place a kiss on Dawn's forehead.

"Dorie?"

"She . . . she's gone."

He sat on the edge of the bed and gathered the two of them into his arms. Wrapping himself around both mother and child, he held them as close as he could. Dorie's tears wet his shirt as the emotion she had been holding in finally exploded. When her grief lessened some, he eased her back against the pillows but kept his hands on her arms.

"I . . . I need to call the funeral home," she said.

"Let me do that for you."

"Order the best. The very best."

"Yes."

"None of it, none of the bad stuff, had to do with her. She is innocent." She looked up at Jonah's face, as if seeking his approval.

"I agree. She was the victim in all of this."

"Yes." She looked back at the baby.

"I'll go call now. Will you be all right?"

"Yes."

"Do you want me to put Dawn in her bassinet?"

"No. I want to hold her as long as I can."

When he left the room and went downstairs, he entered the living room, where Annie and Sarah were listening to the radio. "Annie, Dorie needs you." When she followed him into the hallway, he told her what had happened. "I'm going to the office to use the telephone. I forgot to ask Dorie where she wants Dawn buried, though."

"She'll want her in the cemetery at Mount Ivy Church, where her parents and her brother are buried."

"I'll take care of it."

Annie went upstairs. Jonah first called the doctor, who said he would be right out. "But there is nothing you can do now, Doctor Porter."

"I'll need to see the baby to issue the death certificate. Only a formality, you understand."

"Yes, of course."

"And I'll give Dorie something to help her sleep."

"That's a good idea. She is very upset."

When he finished the conversation, he called the funeral home.

"Be assured we'll treat the loved one with dignity."

"We want the finest infant casket you have."

"I'll see to it personally. Do you know yet what day you want the funeral?"

"No. I'll have to talk to my wife about that. Perhaps in two or three days?"

"That would be fine with us. This is, let's see, this is Thursday evening. So we're talking about Saturday? We don't schedule Sunday services. There is a conflict with the regular Sunday activities. Or we could wait until Monday."

"Saturday will be fine. If my wife has a different idea, I'll call you back."

"Who will be conducting the service?"

"Do you happen to know who did the services for my wife's parents and brother?"

"I believe the pastor of Mount Ivy Church, Reverend Lattimore, conducted the services for Bigelow Barnett and his son, Bixby. He is still the pastor there. Mrs. Barnett died some time previous to that. Old Reverend Holcomb was the pastor then, but he has passed since that time."

"I'll check with her tomorrow and let you know if she changes anything, and I'll get in touch with Reverend Lattimore."

"May we come pick up the deceased now? Has a doctor issued the death certificate yet?"

"I just got off the phone with him. He'll be here shortly."

"If you'll give me a call back when he leaves, we'll be on out then. I assume you don't want the viewing in the home?"

"We don't want a viewing at all."

"That might be best. No need to have people traipsing in to see a baby they never knew."

"Exactly. Just a bunch of voyeurs. I imagine it will just be my wife and myself and a few people from the Big B at the service."

When Jonah returned to the living room, Sarah was rearranging the furniture in her dollhouse and listening to the radio. She looked up when he entered the room.

"Sarah, come sit in my lap so I can talk to you."

She climbed up and looked into his somber face. "Sarah, I have some bad news."

"What is it?" she asked warily.

"The baby died. She was born too early, and she wasn't big enough to live outside Dorie's belly."

"Oh!" She looked sad. Her eyes filled with tears. "So I won't have a sister?"

"No. I'm afraid not." He was on the verge of saying, "Maybe later, in a year or two," but he stopped himself. There was no year or two for Dorie and him. There were only about another five months left in their marriage. It was at that moment it occurred to him that he didn't want it to be over after the year was up.

It would be up to him to take care of the matter of his sister's marriage and death, but after that, he would be free to live his life as he wanted, and what he wanted was to rid Dorie of her molester, her enemy, for once and for all. Then he wanted a real marriage before a pastor, not a rushed ceremony by a justice of the peace who had been bribed to ignore the law. He wanted Dorie for his real wife, not just a pretend one. He wanted the three of them, and Annie, of course, to be a real family.

Chapter 30

"Annie, do you know where my mother's Bible is?" Dorie asked.

"Hmm. I don't think I do, but I'll look for it." She paused from folding and putting the baby clothes in a box. "I thought it was in the bottom drawer of your bureau."

"Maybe it is. I look when I next get up."

"You just stay in bed. I'll look for it."

Jonah and Sarah appeared at the bedroom door. "What are you looking for?" he asked.

"My mother's Bible."

"I have *my* mother's Bible," Sarah chimed in. "Do you want to see it?"

"I remember. We read the Christmas story from it." Dorie smiled at the memory.

"Do you want to read another story?"

"Not this time. I want to record Dawn's birth and . . ." Dorie's voice broke. "I want to put the date in the Bible. That's what you do when somebody is born or dies."

"Is my birthday in the Bible that was my mother's?" She looked up at Jonah.

"I imagine it is, Punkin. Why don't you look and see?"

She disappeared down the hall toward her room.

"Here, Miss Dorie. It was in the bottom drawer, along with a bunch of pictures and clippings from the newspaper." Annie took the large, black book to the bed.

"I'll need a fountain pen from the office."

"I'll get one for you," Jonah said. He turned to go fetch one, but Sarah returned at that moment.

"Uncle Jonah, show me where my name is. Show me where my mama put it in the Bible."

"It was probably your grandmother who wrote it," he explained. "She was proud of keeping all the important dates in here. I was surprised she let your mother have it." He thumbed through the pages until he came to the center section, which held a long list of births, marriages, and deaths. "See, right here is your name and the date you were born."

He was trying to balance the heavy book and hold his finger on the spot where Sarah's birth was recorded when the book slipped and tumbled to the floor. He held back a mild curse as the book landed upside down and open. When he picked it up, the back cover and the lining had become separated, and the lining was folded back at the corner.

"This looks like it's been glued together before and the glue didn't hold," he said. A corner of something white peeked out. Carefully, he grasped an edge with two fingers and gently tugged. The opening wasn't large enough to retrieve whatever was inside, so he cautiously stuck his finger under the edge and pulled more of the lining loose.

The square of paper inside slid out easily. Jonah walked toward the bed and placed the Bible on the foot then unfolded the document. A smile lit his face. "It's what I've been looking for! What those men were looking for! And it's been right here all this time."

"What is it, Uncle Jonah?"

"A marriage license, Punkin. The license from when your mother and father got married."

"And it's good to find it?"

"It's very good to find it!"

If there is a body, there'll be a funeral, he thought. *And that's the perfect place to offer assistance to the grieving widow.*

He slid the telephone in front of him and took the earpiece from the hook on the side. "Operator, give me Fentress Funeral Home."

A few seconds later, they answered. Now he would know.

"Could you tell me when the Crandall funeral is scheduled?"

"The Crandall service is at 10 am tomorrow, Saturday, at Mount Ivy Chapel. There is no viewing scheduled."

"Thank you." He was smiling when he hung up. Everything was back on track. The pregnant widow would need his help in managing the ranch and various businesses. *Dorie will be busy with a new baby in a few months. Navco Oil is on schedule with the drilling on my land where it directly adjoins hers. It will be easy enough to take care of the paperwork involved in transferring a piece of property from her name to mine, at least until we married and the whole thing becomes mine, if not in name, then in practice. A husband has rights, after all, to his wife's assets. Or I'll see that it works that way.*

The engineers in charge of drilling on his land were very certain the oil field ran from a small area on his property to a much larger area on the Big B. He leaned back in his chair and dreamed of how rich he would be when the gushers came in on what, by then, would be his property.

Chapter 31

Dorie didn't say a word when Jonah took the wheel of her beloved Speedster. He didn't want to be an overbearing husband, but he was afraid he would have had to be in that situation. Driving took a certain amount of strength, and Dorie had none after the wreck and subsequent birth.

Sarah rode with Annie and Crippled Elk in his truck. He was hesitant about going to the funeral, but Annie said, "We are Miss Dorie's family, and family goes to family funerals."

Most of the cowboys from the Big B were there. They crammed into the few trucks available, and some even rode horses to the small church. The building was old enough that there was still a hitching rail in front. Although it was seldom used anymore, it came in handy that day.

When Jonah pulled up in front, Dorie was surprised by the number of vehicles present. "Word gets around," Jonah said. "It's not like this was a secret." He got out and went around to the passenger side. "Let me help you, now. You're still weak."

"Not so much weak as sore. I'm still aching from the wreck, and it's hard to move. I'm getting better, though."

She leaned against him as they walked to the church. Reverend Lattimore was standing at the double front doors, which were thrown open to welcome people to the church. "Mrs. Crandall," he said as he drew her into his open arms, "my prayers are with you on this day. You and Mr. Crandall take a seat in the front pew. Mrs. Runningdeer and Mister . . . er . . . her companion are there already, along with the child."

The minister had been to the Big House the day before, and he and Dorie had talked about the service. He had asked what her favorite scripture was, to which she replied, "The Twenty-third Psalm."

"I believe that I read it at your brother's funeral, also."

"Yes, you did. It always comforts me." Dorie didn't make any suggestions for her father's funeral service. It had been up to the minister to choose appropriate words for the death of a man who considered himself boss and commander of his family and all he surveyed. His message centered on the fact that the Lord works in mysterious ways.

Dorie and Jonah took their places in the front pew. A small casket sat on a stand just in front of the pulpit. It was covered with flowers, the spray so large that it spilled over the sides, almost to the floor in places. There was a variety of flowers and every color in the rainbow: pink and red carnations, orange cosmos, blue and purple larkspur, even green blooms and white baby's-breath.

"I hope you like the flowers," Jonah said. "You said to tell the florist to make it the most beautiful they had ever done."

Dorie held him close to her, her arm through his and her other hand gripping his hand. "It's glorious, almost like a field of wildflowers—wildflowers she will never see." Tears threatened to spill, and she tightened her hold on him. His hand was over hers, and he gave a squeeze. She looked up at his face. "I'm so glad I have you here. I couldn't have gone through it without you."

She wouldn't have had to go through it without me, since the whole reason Dawn was born too early and died was because someone was trying to kill me, he thought, but it was better not to mention that fact.

People were still arriving. He didn't turn to see, but he knew the crew from the Big B filled about a third of the pews, and still he heard more folks greeting each other and taking their places. Either the townspeople were curious about what was happening on the Big B Ranch or else Dorie was especially well liked. He bet it was some of both.

Finally, Reverend Lattimore came to the front of the room and mounted the platform. "Please, if everyone would slide toward the inside and leave places for latecomers, it would make it easier for them to find seats. Thank you."

Then he started speaking. He talked about how loved Dorie was in the community. He talked about a mother's love for her child, how that child would always have a place in her heart, and how a mother would do anything for her child.

Jonah's mind went to his sister and how she had wanted to protect Sarah. He thought about how Letty had told Sarah to hide if anyone came, and that advice had saved Sarah's life. He thought about how much he loved Sarah and how much he loved Dorie.

By the time he started listening to Reverend Lattimore again, the minister had moved on to God's love for mankind. Jonah heard stirs as more people entered and found seats at the rear of the room. Lattimore spoke on comfort and support. He ended with the scripture Dorie had chosen. "Lo, though I walk through the valley of death, I will fear no evil." He ended the service with prayer.

In the rear of the church, the latecomers had slid into the pews just as the reverend started on God's love for man. Judge Blackmon nudged Grainger's arm. "Say, that's a mighty small casket for a man, isn't it?"

"Shh. . ." The judge's wife put her hand on his arm.

Grainger peered this way and that but couldn't see around the big hat worn by the woman in front of him. On the other side of the judge's wife sat their obviously pregnant daughter, and on the aisle seat sat Lon Grainger, Junior.

When the prayer ended, Reverend Lattimore said, "We will meet in the cemetery adjoining the church in ten minutes for the interment. After that, the Ladies Aide Society will serve luncheon in the fellowship hall.

Chapter 32

"That was a lovely prayer," Dorie said, wiping her eyes with her lace-trimmed hankie.

"Dorie, dear," said the woman who approached with outstretched arms. "I am so sorry about your loss. I didn't even know you were expecting. I had only recently learned that you had married." She hugged Dorie. Stepping back, she gave Jonah an appraising stare.

"We were married last summer," he said, trying to set the record straight.

"Oh?" She looked doubtful, as if he would make up something like that.

"A beautiful service," said the second woman, and the sentiment was repeated by the third and fourth.

Sarah climbed onto the pew seat and held up her arms to be picked up. Jonah gathered her into his arms, and she turned to look out over the crowd. "Papa!" she yelled. She turned to Jonah and said, "There's my papa! See him? Back there." She pointed toward the rear of the room. "Let me down!" She took off running as soon as her feet touched the floor.

The crowd around Dorie offering their condolences stared at Sarah's first pronouncement, and several took steps to see better whom she was talking about as she raced toward the man she had spotted.

"Papa! Papa!" She worked her way through the crowd in the aisle until she reached the last pew, where she threw her arms around Lon Grainger, Junior's legs. "Why didn't you come back, Papa? We were hungry. Mama and I were hungry, and we didn't have any food. Mama went into the woods to find us some berries to eat, and she didn't come back. I was scared, Papa. I so wished you would come and find me, but you didn't. Two men came, and I was scared of them, so I hid. Mama's dead, Papa. She died in the woods."

The people surrounding the pair were held enthralled by the scene, listening for whatever came next. Even Reverend Lattimore stood in stunned silence. Ignoring his wife, Myrnalee, who was clinging to his arm, eyes wide as she heard Sarah's story, Lonnie turned toward his father, who stood beside Judge Blackmon. "I thought you said you had taken care of this . . . this problem. I thought you paid plenty of money to set them up someplace where they wouldn't get in the way."

"I did! I paid plenty to solve your problem, just like I've done all your life!"

Jonah had followed Sarah up the aisle and heard the whole exchange.

"He paid two men to kill them, is what he did, or else you did."

The whole church full of people gasped.

"I didn't pay anyone to kill them!" Lonnie exclaimed. "I didn't want them dead. I just wanted them to go away."

"Who is this man?" the judge asked. "Who is this making these accusations?"

"I'm his wife's brother," Jonah answered.

"I don't have a brother," said the woman trying to hold on to the younger Grainger's arm.

"No," agreed the judge. At the same time, a gray-headed woman who had her hands resting on the younger woman's shoulders said, "Myrnalee doesn't have a brother."

"But Myrnalee isn't his wife," Jonah retorted. The young woman's knees gave way, and she collapsed onto a pew.

"She most certainly is his wife. I married them myself," Judge Blackmon said.

"He was married to someone else when you performed that ceremony, so it wasn't a valid marriage."

"That's a lie!" Lon Senior declared. "There is no proof!"

"I can prove it," Jonah retorted.

"How? How can you prove it?"

"I have the marriage license. The men he, or you, sent to kill them didn't find it. I did, and I have it in a safe place. He was married to my sister, Letitia Crandall, at the time of the so-called marriage to this woman."

"That's bigamy," a voice could be heard from the crowd.

"You can go to jail for that," said a second voice.

Lonnie was sweating, drops falling from his forehead. He looked desperately at his father.

"It's not as bad a crime as murder," Jonah said. "One of these men paid two killers to do away with any evidence of a prior marriage. They shot my sister and left her body in the woods. Sarah hid, so they didn't find her, else she would be dead, too."

The murmurs grew. "Somebody send for the sheriff," a voice called out.

Chapter 33

Dorie had collapsed onto the front pew. She was turned to the side, watching the commotion in the back of the church. When Jonah saw her, he said, "My wife has had enough of this. Reverend, can we finish the services so I can get her home? This is the first time she has been out of bed, and she needs to get back there."

"Certainly, Mr. Crandall, certainly." He scanned the crowd of buzzing onlookers. "Everyone gather outside." He spoke loudly enough that everyone in the sanctuary could hear him. "Baby Dawn Crandall will be interred beside her grandparents in the churchyard." Everyone except the Grainger entourage exited and gathered around the gravesite for the brief ceremony. By the time it was over, Dorie was pale and shaking. "You'll excuse us, Reverend, if we don't stay for the meal. I'm afraid my wife cannot bear any more today."

"I understand. If you need anything, anything at all, just call."

Their actions had no bearing on the rest of the people at the church. They were all ready to meet, eat, and talk about the scandalous accusations that had been thrown about, and they wanted to be there to see what would happen when the sheriff showed up. Someone went to a nearby house to use the telephone to call him.

As soon as they got to the Big House, Jonah gathered Dorie in his arms and carried her up the stairs. "Don't! I'm too heavy. You'll hurt your back," she said.

"You? Heavy?" He smiled at her. "You weigh about as much as a little puff of dandelion fluff." He carefully placed

THE MARRIAGE BARGAIN | 156

her on her bed, and his smile disappeared. "I'm sorry Dawn's service was interrupted like that."

"I'm not!"

"You're not?"

"No. Something had to be done, and I'm sure Sarah feels better for getting it all out in the open. She needed to tell her father what went on when he left them alone like that." She used her toes to push off her shoes, which hit the floor with a thud.

"Yes, he needed to know, but I don't expect that he cared much about it. If he cared, he would have never left them like that in the first place." He eased Dorie back onto the pillows and pulled a blanket up over her then went to the chair and sat down. "He never would have put them out there in the country with nobody around for miles, if he cared for them. He would have taken his wife and child to live in his hometown, where they would have been known as his wife and daughter."

"You're right about that. I can't begin to guess why he kept it secret in the first place, unless it was because he thought his father wouldn't approve. Now that I know that Lonnie Grainger is Sarah's father, that makes sense. I expect Lonnie got mixed up with Judge Blackmon's daughter at Lon's urging, married her to make his father happy and didn't know how to handle it." She sat up and adjusted the blanket so it covered her feet.

"If what I heard today is to be believed, his father knew about the marriage to Letty. He's the one who sent the men to get rid of her."

"That's just about the most exciting funeral I ever been to," Annie said as she entered the room. "Little Bird, she wanted to stay and eat, but I reckoned it was better to come back to the Big House. She talked about it all the way home. Done her some good to get all that out of her mouth."

They heard the pounding of steps as Sarah rushed up the stairs. "That was my papa, Dorie."

"*Miss* Dorie," Annie corrected.

"Miss Dorie, that was my papa. I told him. I told him he should have come for us. He should have seen to it we had food. I told him we were hungry and that I was scared. He ought to know that, oughtn't he?" She looked first at Dorie, then at Jonah.

"Yes, Punkin, he sure ought to know that. He should have taken care of his little girl."

"I don't want to be his little girl any more, Uncle Jonah. I want to be your little girl."

"That's what I want, too, Punkin. I want you to be my little girl."

"Forever and ever?"

"Yes. Forever and ever." He looked at Dorie, but she glanced away, avoiding his gaze.

"Come, Little Bird, we missed the lunch. Let's go fix us something, and we'll fix a tray for Miss Dorie."

"I'll bet there were lots of pies and cakes there, Annie. I wish we could have stayed," Jonah heard her say as they went down the stairs.

Jonah and Dorie remained silent. Neither knew exactly what to say or what the revelations of the day would do to them or others. Finally, Jonah rose from the bed. "Guess I'll go get something to eat, too. Should I bring you something?"

"Annie said she'll bring a tray. I'll wait on that, or maybe just take a nap."

Long after Jonah left the room, Dorie thought about the fact that she might not need this so-called marriage much longer. If Lon Grainger were jailed for his part in any of this, she would be free of him. She wouldn't need Jonah's name to protect her any longer, but she wanted it. She wanted *him*. And she wanted Sarah to be her little girl. Forever and ever.

Chapter 34

Three hours later, the sheriff called and asked if he could come by and talk to them. "You can certainly talk to me, Sheriff. My wife is sleeping. It's been a difficult few days for her. When you come, I'll see if she's awake and strong enough to speak to you."

When the lawman arrived, Annie took Sarah out to the chicken coop to look for eggs so she wouldn't overhear the conversation about the terrible things her father and grandfather had done. Jonah took the sheriff into the office and shut the door. He told all about Letty's handicap and the furtive marriage. He showed him the marriage license he had found hidden in the lining of the family Bible.

"So they really were married," the sheriff said. "It wasn't some kind of bogus setup to make her think they were."

"No, it wasn't. Letty and Sarah lived with my parents for the first few years of Sarah's life, with Grainger popping in and out, until my father put his foot down and demanded that Lonnie take care of his family. Letty had given my mother the marriage license when they returned home, and my mother put it away for safekeeping.

"Now that I think about it, I remember Lonnie saying, 'Now you have the marriage license in a safe place, don't you?' I reckon he was expecting her to tell him where it was so he could get it and destroy it."

"Neither Lonnie nor Lon have said much about that part," the sheriff mused. "Lonnie has said that his father was furious when he found out about the marriage. They had a problem doing away with it, though. If Lonnie had filed for a divorce, he would have had to give cause, and there would be records about all that. More records that would lead back to the marriage. So Lonnie set up housekeeping for your sister someplace he thought nobody would ever find her." He shook his head as he discussed the actions of the younger man.

"It was sure remote. I'll give you that. And when she wrote our mother, there was no address she could put on it, only that she lived in a cute little house by the edge of the woods. Turned out it was near The Thicket."

The sheriff shook his head again. "That's one scary part of the country. It's so full of snakes and bears and panthers that grown men are afraid to go there. I think it even scares the rascals who hide from the law in there."

Jonah took up the story. "At first, according to letters Mother received, Lonnie came often and brought money and presents. The neighbors kept watch and bought groceries for Letty and Sarah and mailed letters for her. Then it came to a stop."

"Most likely that's when Lon decided Lonnie should marry Judge Blackmon's daughter, Myrnalee. Lonnie told me that Lon said he'd take care of the first wife by buying her a nice home and setting up a fund to pay her money to live on in fine style if she promised to never tell about the marriage."

"Instead, he sent two men to kill her."

"I don't think Lonnie knew about that part. I don't know that he would have gone for something like that."

"Like father, like son," Jonah said.

"Maybe."

"Well, he sure could have let her starve to death—her and Sarah. There was no food in the house and no money to buy any. Letty went into the woods to find plums and berries to eat." Furious at the idea, Jonah stood up and paced the room.

"In The Thicket, that would have been a death sentence, anyway."

"Yes. If the men had not found and shot her, likely the wild animals would have done it for them."

"How do you think the little girl escaped them?"

"I've thought about that. Maybe Grainger only mentioned the wife, and they didn't know about her. Maybe Lonnie didn't tell his father about having a daughter. Or maybe they knew about her, but when they didn't see her, they thought she went into the woods with Letty and was lost or dead. We'll never know what Letty said to them before she died." Jonah stopped before his voice broke. He rubbed his eyes, pausing before he continued.

"You told me the child said her mother told her if anyone came around to hide. You reckon she knew something bad was going to happen?" the sheriff speculated.

"Could be, Sheriff. Could be. Sometimes Letty surprised us with things she figured out. It's like she had a special sense of knowing things others didn't."

"You know I'll have to check all this out with the sheriff down there where she died, don't you?"

"Yes. I know. That's fine. I only ask that you don't bother my parents. They don't know all this, only that Letty is dead. I didn't tell them how or why. I want to be the one to tell them, and it'll be a while before I can do that."

"That's fair enough. They don't know anything about this from the time your sister left their home. Is that right?"

"Yes, Sheriff, that's right. They only know that she and Sarah lived in a small house at the edge of the forest and that Lonnie came to see them and that he stopped coming. I only wrote to tell them that Letty was dead and that Sarah was safe with me, but I didn't tell them where I was, in case Grainger showed up at their place looking for her."

"I don't know that I'll need to contact them, unless I need to find out what was in the letters your sister sent home. Now"—he sat back and looked at Jonah—"let's talk about what went on here in this county."

Chapter 35

"Where should I start?"

"At the beginning. That's the best place. What were you doing here? Here in this county, that is."

"I looked for Grainger, and this is where I found him, in Cottonport."

"What were you going to do when you found him?"

"I don't know, Sheriff. I really don't know." Jonah sat back down. "I'm not a killing man, although I'll admit the idea crossed my mind." He looked the sheriff in the eye. "I'm not saying I would have done it. Though, I was scheming how I could bring him to justice for what he did to my sister—how I could embarrass him, ruin his life, destroy him—but I had no idea how to do it. Especially since at the time I couldn't find the marriage license that would prove what I said was true."

"So what *were* you doing?"

"I had Sarah stashed away in the next county. I didn't want Grainger to be able to find her. Her life would have been in danger if he knew she was still alive. I figured the first place he'd look was at my parents' home, so I couldn't take her there."

"Which Grainger? Senior or Junior?"

"Either one. At the time, I thought it was Junior who had hired the killers. After all, she was married to Junior—Lonnie."

"Go on."

"I got a job here on the Big B."

"Are you a cowboy? A wrangler? What?"

Jonah laughed. "Actually, I hadn't done any ranch work since I was a kid. I work at my father's bank."

"Your father's bank?" He sat up straighter and eyed Jonah. "You're a banker?"

"Yes, Sheriff, my father's bank. Actually, he owns a lot of businesses, and I'm involved with several of them. I set all that aside to find out what happened to my sister and niece. I worked on the family ranch when I was in my teens, so I knew enough to get by."

"And you got a job on the Big B."

"Yes. I worked around the spread, mending fences and doing chores, and when I could I went into town and sat in the bars, and I listened and learned. I learned that Lonnie Grainger had married the judge's daughter—except it wasn't a marriage, because he was still married to Letty at the time of the second ceremony."

"Which he probably didn't know."

"Maybe not, if he thought his father had arranged a divorce in some way." He frowned at the thought.

"How did you end up married to Dorie Barnett?"

"The usual way, Sheriff. The usual way." *I'm not going into details about Dorie's unusual proposal. That doesn't enter into it, and I won't embarrass my wife with the particulars of the bargain. If she wants the sheriff to know about the rape and pregnancy, she can tell him herself.*

"No one around here knew about the marriage until after the fact."

"No. We went to Galveston and got married there. Had the honeymoon at the same time, so to speak."

"And kept to yourself. Kept it a secret."

"No, Sheriff. We didn't keep it a secret. We saw people in Galveston who were from Cottonport. They knew, and I'm sure they spread the word. We just stayed on the ranch, working. I went and got my niece and brought her here to live with us. We had plenty on the Big B to keep us busy, and neither one of us are socializing types."

The sheriff frowned and leaned forward, resting his elbows on his knees. "Tell me about these attempts on your life."

Jonah wondered who had told him about those. "Well, Sheriff, you have to understand some background—why we think someone was trying to kill me."

The sheriff looked up. "Tell me."

"Lon Grainger, Senior, that is, not Junior, was after Dorie to marry him. She didn't want to. He wouldn't take no for an answer. He was more than insistent, said she would marry him, sooner rather than later, he'd see to it. That's one reason we went to Galveston to get married. No interference. We did it, and it was done.

"I guess it's common knowledge that Navco Oil is drilling on Grainger's land, right at the place where his land meets Dorie's. It was plain—at least to Dorie—that he was after her land. She wouldn't sell, so the next best thing was to marry her and take over. *If that had happened, it wouldn't have been long before Dorie died in some unfortunate accident, but I have no proof of that, only a feeling fueled by the things that go on around whatever Grainger has anything to do with.*

"I don't know if you or your wife knew, but he got the property he owns now through marriage. Lonnie's mother inherited it from her father."

"No, I didn't know that. I don't know if Dorie did or not. Anyway, not long after we married, the hands started seeing signs of someone poking around the place. Horse prints and boot prints in places where nobody should have been. Catching sight of a stranger trying to stay out of view. Cigarette butts where none of our men had been. Things like that."

"That doesn't point to someone trying to kill you," the sheriff commented.

"No, but shooting through our front window does."

The sheriff's eyebrows raised. "I'd say so! When did this happen?"

"Not long before Christmas. We were sitting in the living room, and I leaned over to see something Sarah wanted to show me. That's when it happened. If I hadn't leaned over, I'd have been a dead man."

The sheriff jumped to his feet. "Good God, man! Didn't you ever think about reporting it to me?"

"No, Sheriff, I didn't. If it was possible to catch the shooter, the fellows on the Big B could do it. This is a capable bunch of hands. If they can't catch him, no one can."

The sheriff's eyes opened wide. "I guess you couldn't figure out who did it."

"No, we didn't. Next day, at daylight, we nosed around. The shot had to have come from fairly close to the house, not only for accuracy, but because the overhang of the porch roof cut down the ease of getting a bead on someone through the window."

"Did you find anything?" He paced up and down the room.

"Just what we had found before. Hoof prints. Boot prints. We started keeping all the drapes and curtains closed all the time."

"Any more shots?"

"No. Not that."

"Then something else?"

"I'll say. A few days ago, they kidnapped Sarah."

The sheriff sighed and regained his seat. "It just keeps getting worse." He shook his head once more. "And, of course, you didn't call me about this."

"It all happened so quickly, Sheriff. We reacted immediately, and it almost cost Dorie her life. It did cost her . . . our baby her life."

"Tell me about it." He settled back for the next harrowing part of the tale.

Chapter 36

"Let me ask you this, Sheriff. Do you know Mr. and Mrs. Cotton? She does ironing for folks, and he picks up and delivers."

"Agnes and Woodrow Cotton. Folks call him Wooley, 'cause of his name and his white hair. Yeah, I know them. What in the world do they have to do with this mess? You'll never convince me that they had anything to do with trying to kill somebody."

"Mrs. Cotton does our ironing. Every week Wooley picks up and delivers here. About a month ago, a man showed up, said he was Wooley's nephew and that Wooley had broken his ankle, so he was filling in until it healed. Annie didn't think anything about it. Next week, same thing."

"What did this fellow look like?"

"That's the thing about it, Sheriff. It's been cold, and the man was bundled up with a cap and scarf all around his face. I never saw him, but Annie says she couldn't rightly give a description, other than he was average height and size. Nothing special about him.

"But the last time he came—that was last Wednesday— he said he had some more ironing in the van and asked Sarah to come let him hand it to her. When she got inside, he clamped a rag with chloroform on it over her nose. When she passed out, quick as a rattlesnake he drove off with her in the van."

"What in the world did he want with the girl? Did Grainger figure out where she was?"

"That's what I thought, at first. But they didn't want her at all. They wanted to draw me away from the house. They knew I'd come chasing after her."

"And did you?"

"Yes, but Dorie beat me to it. She was out the door in a flash. Annie came screaming for us, and before I could get from the office where I was working to the back door, Dorie was gone. My truck was parked out back, and she jumped in it and took off after him. I had to go into the barn to get her car, so I was way behind, but I caught up fast, driving the Speedster."

The sheriff scratched his head. "I don't know that I'm seeing where this is going. If they were after you, how did your wife get hurt?"

"She was in my truck, Sheriff, and dressed in men's clothes, to boot. She followed Cotton's van onto the road that follows along the river. That's when another truck pulled out from behind some bushes. He ran up right behind her and started ramming her. I could see it happening, but I was still a good ways back. He pulled up beside my truck and shoved her off the road. The truck rolled over and over until it ended up in the Brazos, upside down."

"Lord, Lord! It's a wonder she survived."

"The driver of the truck that rammed her, he stayed long enough to see her go into the river then took off. By then, I was there. I ran down the bank to where she was."

"And you got her out!"

"Yes. We were lucky. There was a big willow tree up almost to the bank, and it held my truck in the shallow water long enough to get her out. Crippled Elk took off right behind me, only slower, and when he caught up, between the two of us we managed to get the door open and ease Dorie out before the truck pushed the tree on out into the Brazos and sank."

"What makes you think those people weren't after her?"

"Why? There was no reason to want her dead. There was a good reason to want to make her a widow."

"I see your point."

"And she was in my truck. Anyone would have thought it was me driving." Jonah had to stop for a moment to compose himself. The thought of Dorie in that truck in the river still sent chills running through him.

"When I got her back to the Big House and cleaned her up and called the doctor, she was in labor."

"And that's how come the baby came so early it couldn't live."

"That's it."

He mulled over all he had been told then asked, "How did you come to get your little girl back?"

"Wooley Cotton called, said he had gone to his van and found her, still asleep from the chloroform."

The sheriff stood and started pacing. "How in the hell did Wooley Cotton get mixed up in all this? Is he kin to these rascals? Was it really his nephew who did this?"

"He didn't know them at all. They came to his house and threatened him and Mrs. Cotton if they didn't cooperate. Every week they came by and took his truck and our ironing. I reckon they were looking over this place and plotting how to do it."

"Well, it sure worked, all right."

"Yes, it did. We're just fortunate they didn't hurt Sarah. She was just the pawn to draw me off the property, and when they were through with her, they left her, unharmed."

"Lucky is right."

"You might get a good description of the man from Wooley or Mrs. Cotton. They must have gotten a good look at them at some point, but they wouldn't tell me. You being the law, they might be more cooperative with you."

The sheriff stood with his hand on the back of the chair. "I'll go check with them next." He shook his head. "This is getting more complicated by the minute. What in the world does killing you have to do with killing your sister? How could they be tied together?"

"I don't know, Sheriff. Maybe they aren't. Or maybe they think I've found information that will lead to Letty's killers, and they want to kill me before I can find them. Or maybe Dorie is right, and Lon Grainger wanted to make her a widow so he could move in and take over."

Chapter 37

Dorie's bruises, the ones people could see, gradually faded. The hurt inside was harder to deal with. Not the physical hurt. Dorie's body was young and healthy and mended quickly, but her emotions, her heart, were a different story.

She hadn't expected to feel the deep sorrow over the loss of the baby she had never wanted, but somehow it wouldn't go away. "How did I go from being so angry and unwilling to be pregnant to this . . . this regret over Dawn's death?" she asked Annie one day as she sat in the homey kitchen, watching the preparations for dinner.

"People—good people like you—do not place blame on the innocent, like your baby. Dawn, she did nothing bad. It was an evil man who planted her in you, but that had nothing to do with your daughter. It was not her fault he did that. It was an evil man who took her from you. You realize this, in your heart, but maybe you feel guilty that you did not want her at first."

"Yes, maybe I do feel guilty about not wanting her, but it's more than that, much more. I have such a sense of loss. Once I saw her, she was mine, and I wanted her completely."

"You had prepared for the baby's arrival. She had already found a place in your heart, and now that place is empty." Annie added the vegetables she had been cutting to the pot of bubbling broth on the range. "Don't worry. You will fill it again." She walked to the refrigerator. "You will fill it with love."

"I doubt it." Dorie rose to her feet.

"Ah . . . you have handsome husband and plenty of time. You will make a new baby. Or even the same baby in a new body."

Dorie paused on her way to the back door. "What do you mean 'same baby in a new body'?"

"Dawn, before she enter the little one in your belly, she was a spirit. She dwelled in the spirit world with Unequa, the Great Spirit. Then came the time she entered the body of one you named Dawn."

Dorie stood, hand on the doorframe.

"The baby was born before her time, and you called her Dawn, but the body, it was not ready to come into this world. The spirit decided it was not time to come from the spirit world into this world, because the body where it was to live was not ready, so spirit go back to live with Unequa."

"I understand that, I guess."

"But some day, you and husband will make a new baby, and a spirit will decide to come live in that baby. Maybe is Dawn, maybe not. Maybe a different spirit."

"Annie, you of all people know that Jonah and I do not have a real marriage."

Annie was silent, stirring the contents of the big pot on the stove.

"When all of this is over, after the trials, the marriage will be over, too."

"Is this what you want? You want marriage to be over?"

"What I want is beside the point. Jonah and I had an agreement, a marriage bargain. He understood why we were marrying, and it wasn't for . . ." She started to say "for love," but things were different than when they had entered into this pact. She had fallen in love. *Not that it would do me any good. I'm an old maid, a woman who had to buy her husband, but only for a year.*

"Maybe . . . maybe not." Annie could be aggravatingly enigmatic.

Dorie left before she was tempted to let her mind wander toward what it would be like if Jonah felt the same way.

Chapter 38

Two months passed before they received word from the court that the trials of both Lon and Lonnie Grainger were coming up shortly. The last of winter had gone, and spring was in full bloom. The rose that bloomed by the back door was full of pink blossoms, and Annie took the dried seed pods she had saved from the previous year and broke them open in the soil beside the car barn door, where they were pushing up tiny green sprouts.

Crippled Elk was working the garden in earnest, and they were eating the results on the dinner table each evening. Spinach, lettuce, and asparagus were served daily, and he said there would be broccoli soon. Sarah had taken to following him around the plots of vegetables, learning from him as she did from Annie.

Jonah had trouble letting his niece out of his sight, constantly imagining the possibilities of what could happen to her. Crippled Elk tried to reassure him. "I will stay close to Little Bird. No one will come without I see them. I can snatch her up before anyone else and hurry her to safety." Jonah finally gave in and let Sarah go anywhere around the outside of the Big House as long as Annie or Crippled Elk was close by.

"I know I have to start letting her have more freedom," he said one evening as he and Dorie, back to their warm weather pattern, sat on the front porch after supper. "I think that when the trials are over and the Graingers are permanently locked up, I'll feel better about the whole thing, like I can let her out of my sight without worrying."

"You think they will both be convicted?" Dorie picked at a fold in her skirt. She appeared calm on the outside, but inside she was a bundle of nerves over the upcoming ordeal. A private person, the thought of spreading her private life out for all to see was making her increasingly nervous. She knew the whole town was talking about what went on at Dawn's funeral, and the trial would add more for them to gossip about.

"I don't see how they won't be." Jonah gazed out beyond the green of the yard to the distance where the Brazos flowed among the oaks and willows.

"Lonnie, for sure," Dorie agreed. "I mean, it's so obvious that he committed bigamy. You have the proof."

"Yes, and Sarah is proof in herself. I hadn't even realized it myself until I saw them together that day at the church. She's the spitting image of him, with her auburn hair and unusual blue eyes. It had been years since I had seen him, and I had forgotten how much they favor."

"Annie has Crippled Elk take her to town to buy groceries, and she's been hearing the gossip. She says that Lonnie's wife has left him and moved back home, and her father is exploring the law to see if she should file for divorce or whether they aren't married at all in the first place."

Jonah shook his head. "That's another person to feel sorry for—another one of his victims in this mess."

"And Myrnalee's baby. It will be called awful names."

They sat in silence for several minutes, each caught up in their own thoughts. Finally, Jonah spoke. "When the trials are over . . ."

When the trials are over, so will be the marriage. He's going to remind me that the year will be up.

"When the trials are over, while all this is fresh on the mind of the court and the judge, I'm going to file to adopt Sarah."

"Oh! What a good idea!"

"Yes. When she said that about not wanting to be his little girl, wanting to be mine, I decided I ought to make it official."

"That would be reassuring to her."

"Yes, I thought that, too. And . . ." He paused.

"Yes?"

"I don't think there is a way in the world this could ever happen, but if Lonnie ever decided, sometime in the future, that he wanted Sarah, if I had adopted her, there would be no way he could get custody of her."

Dorie snorted. "After all that's happened, there's not a court in Texas that would give her to him."

"I don't think so, either, but it's best not to take chances."

Chapter 39

The next morning, Jonah had just come down the stairs when the telephone rang.

"Mr. Crandall?"

"Speaking."

"This is John Sturgis, Prosecuting Attorney."

"Yes, Mr. Sturgis. How can I help you?"

"I am preparing for the Grainger trial, and I need to meet with you and your wife. Is it possible for you to come to my office today?"

"I'd have to check with my wife to be sure, Mr. Sturgis, but I think we could come into town. Say this afternoon?"

"Afternoon is fine. One o'clock would be good for me."

"Let's say one o'clock then. If my wife has some reason she can't come, I'll let you know."

"I need to speak with both of you."

"I understand."

When Dorie came downstairs a few minutes later, Jonah told her about the call.

"I wonder what he wants," she mused.

"Probably just going over everything one more time."

"Did he tell you when the trials will take place?"

"No, he didn't. We can find out this afternoon."

They had an early lunch and went upstairs to change. Jonah told Dorie to dress as if she were going to meet the governor. "Look like you are rich and important, and you'll get treated that way," he said.

"My father went looking like what he was, a rancher," she replied. "Everyone treated him well."

"Everyone already knew he was rich and important. You need to make sure people know that you are, too."

She changed into a navy blue, slim-fitting dress with a white collar. She pinned a gold and pearl pin to it and donned white gloves. Jonah dressed in one of the suits she had bought him in Houston on their wedding trip.

"We're dressed so fine folks will think we're millionaires," she joked.

"Aren't we?" Jonah replied.

Dorie drove off at a much slower rate than she had the time she and Jonah were headed to Galveston to get married. The recent traumatic wreck had left her with a more cautious attitude toward speed.

"I meant to tell you," she said to Jonah. "Navco Oil called again the other day."

"Oh? What did they want?"

"What they always want—to talk to me about drilling on my land."

"Are you going to let them?"

"I'm thinking about it." She waited for him to comment, but he didn't. Finally, she said, "I'd like to talk to you about it sometime."

He turned to her, eyebrows raised. "OK. Anytime you want."

They were silent the rest of the way to town.

John Sturgis was dressed much like Jonah, in a dark suit, white dress shirt, and a striped tie. Dorie was glad her husband had suggested dressing the part of a rich, important, businesslike ranch owner. It helped her feel more like an equal of the tall, bald-headed man behind the imposing desk; otherwise, she might have felt like a little girl before this authoritative man.

"Mrs. Crandall, Mr. Crandall, have a seat, please." He motioned toward the two chairs in front of his desk. Dorie looked around at the office. Formal, well-furnished, not what she had expected, not that she had any idea of what to expect. It could have been the office of a prominent businessman.

He took his seat also. "We are planning to go to trial in about two weeks. It has taken some time to find a judge to preside over the proceedings."

"Oh?" This surprised her.

"Due to the persons involved, Judge Blackmon recused himself, and it took a while to find another judge who could or would leave his own courtroom for a while."

"I hadn't thought about that."

"I assume there will be two separate trials," Jonah said.

"Well, no. We have come to an agreement."

"An agreement?" Dorie and Jonah said in unison. "What kind of an agreement," Jonah asked, frowning.

"First, let me tell you that we still have both Graingers in jail."

"Good," Jonah murmured.

"There was too big a chance they would leave, not only the county, but the state and maybe the country."

"So what's the deal?" Jonah asked.

"In order to prove that Lon Senior was behind the killing of your sister, we need the testimony of Lon Junior—Lonnie. We have quite a few witnesses to what was said at the church. Lots of people heard it, but the defense could twist that around any which way. We needed something even better—Lonnie's testimony of what went on about his marriage, what his father knew, what his father said to him, what he thought his father was going to do."

"And what did he think his father was going to do?"

"Get him a divorce, quietly, privately, and buy off your sister with a house and money. Lon Senior, you see, thought Lonnie had already taken care of it in that way. It wasn't until after Lonnie and Myrnalee had married that Lonnie fessed up to his father what he had really done—set up your sister in a house where he could visit her when he wanted, and that they were still married."

"So Lon . . ."

"Lon knew that might not take care of the problem, especially the bigamy. As long as your sister was still alive, there was always a chance of the whole thing being found out. He decided to solve it a different way."

"By having her killed."

"Right."

"And Lonnie's child? Grainger's grandchild?" Dorie was especially bothered by the thought that Lon would have his grandchild murdered.

"I don't know if Lonnie ever told his father about the child. Lon says he didn't know about Sarah, and that is backed up by what Lonnie says."

"So she was never in danger?"

"Not until now. Lonnie could have told him at any point, but so far he kept his mouth shut." Sturgis twirled a pen around in his fingers. "Of course, if they had seen Sarah that day . . ." He said no more, but the implication was clear.

Jonah twisted in the chair. "So is she in danger now?"

Sturgis sighed and threw the pen down on the blotter. "I'd like to say no, but I can't be sure. At least until the trial, I'd keep her close. After all, the two men who shot your sister are still out there somewhere, if they haven't left the area, that is, and Sarah saw them."

"But they don't know she exists. Right?"

"You're right, but Grainger does now, when he didn't before. He could pass the word along somehow. After she testifies, we'll rethink it."

"Testifies? Sarah is going to have to testify?" Dorie was appalled.

"She's the only one who can tell about there being two men who came and tore up the house," Sturgis explained. "We need her. She's an important link in the case."

"Tell us about the deal you were talking about."

"We made a bargain with Lonnie. He testifies against his father at the trial, tells all about his marriage to Letty and his father's objections—the whole story from beginning to end—and we'll let him out of jail. After he's testified, of course . . . not until then."

"What about the bigamy charge?"

"Judge Blackmon is researching that. Sometimes people serve a jail sentence for bigamy, sometimes they pay a fine, or both. Of course the judge is out for blood, seeing as how his daughter is the injured party."

"So Lonnie is going to get away with it?"

"No. I'm not saying that. I agreed to not charge him in the murder of your sister if he testifies against his father. I truly think he was under the impression that his father was doing what he said, obtaining a secret divorce and setting Letty up with a house and money. We could never prove that Lonnie knew anything about the murder, anyway. We'd lose that case if we tried to prosecute. But it was a good carrot to get him to testify against Lon Senior. He'll go to trial for the bigamy, for sure. Judge Blackmon will see to it."

"What about the kidnapping?" Dorie asked. "And the people who tried to kill me . . . or Jonah. I'm sure they thought it was Jonah driving his truck."

"I agree, Mrs. Crandall, but that is a separate issue—a separate trial—and I don't have enough evidence to prosecute. Who would I prosecute?"

"Lon Grainger," Jonah said. "He's who is behind it."

"I think so, too, Mr. Crandall, but I have to have proof. I have to have the men who did it."

"That will be hard to accomplish." Jonah shook his head.

"Sarah is the key to that. She's the only one who has seen them."

"And she didn't get a good look at the man who took her."

"I understand, and that's one of the problems with that case."

Jonah frowned. Looking at the floor, he turned his head from side to side. "There was something she said that day when I went to the Cotton's house to get her."

"Pertaining to the man who took her?" Sturgis leaned forward, excited. "What was it?"

"I remember," Jonah finally said. "She said the man who took her might be one of the men who tore up their house."

"Why did she say that?" Sturgis crossed his arms on the desk and stared intently at Jonah.

"I don't know. She changed the subject, and I didn't want to press her after what she had been through that day. I meant to bring it up later, but with the baby coming and all, I forgot about what she had said."

Sturgis leaned back in his chair. "Maybe his voice. Or his eyes." He looked from Jonah to Dorie. "If she mentions anything more about it, remember what she says, but don't question her. I'll do that when I meet and go over what the trial is going to be like with her."

"When will that be?" Dorie asked.

"I think I'll wait until about two days before the trial so it will still be on her mind when the real thing happens."

"I'll prepare her for meeting with you," Jonah said.

"Don't try to prepare her too much," Sturgis cautioned. "Just tell her not to be afraid of me. I'm only going to ask her questions about what happened, nothing she can't answer."

"If it had been right after she came to live with us, she would have been very frightened, I think, but she's a different child now. She'll do fine. Nothing much scares her these days."

Chapter 40

Almost three weeks later, the trial started. The prosecuting attorney had met with Jonah once again, and with Sarah. Dorie was not part of the case, at least not until the point when she might be asked to tell what she saw and heard at Dawn's funeral.

"It won't be necessary for Sarah to be present the first day," Sturgis told them. "Or you either, Mrs. Crandall, for that matter."

"I'll be there to support my husband."

"Yes. That's probably a good idea. It tells the jury that you support and believe him."

"Why wouldn't I?"

"No reason, but the defense will try to make it sound like anything he says is either a lie or he's mixed up."

"Why would they do that?"

"Anything to throw doubt on our case against Grainger."

On the first day of the trial, they met in the hallway at the rear of the courtroom. "Are you ready, Mr. Crandall?" Sturgis asked.

"I should be asking you that question," Jonah joked as they shook hands.

"More than ready," the prosecutor replied. He turned to go into the courtroom but paused to say, "Don't worry. We'll win."

At that moment, a tall man, square and hardy, dressed in a suit and tie, approached from the direction of the stairs. "What in the hell have you got yourself into this time?" He slapped his hand onto Jonah's shoulder.

Turning, Jonah's jaw dropped, and he threw both arms around the stranger. "Thomas! What are you doing here?"

"I got a letter from the prosecuting attorney, John Sturgis. He said I might be needed to testify in a murder trial, that I would be backing up your testimony. So, did you kill somebody, little brother?"

"Thomas," Jonah gripped his brother's arms and held him still. "The trial concerns Letty's murder."

"My God!" Thomas looked stunned. "I read the letter you sent the folks. You said she was dead, not that she had been murdered. What happened? Who did it?"

As Jonah started to speak, Sturgis stuck his head out the courtroom door. "We're fixing to start. Time to come in and get a seat."

"Are you John Sturgis?"

"Yes, I am."

"I'm Thomas Crandall." He offered his hand.

"Mr. Crandall! I'm glad you made it. I had hoped to speak to you first to fill you in on what's happening, unless your brother has already told you."

"No"—he glanced at Jonah—"my brother never tells me anything."

"Well, I don't have time now. You'll see by what goes on in the courtroom. Come on folks. I have seats reserved for you. The place is getting filled up quickly."

They filed down to the front and took seats right behind the prosecutor's table. As they settled into their seats, Thomas put his hand on Jonah's shoulder and said, "Tell me, little brother, who is this charming woman with you?" He smiled broadly at Dorie. "Introduce us. Please."

"Certainly, big brother. This lovely lady is my wife."

Chapter 41

"All rise." The bailiff's words rang out, cutting the voices from a rumble to a hushed buzz as people rose, then sat again. The room was packed. Murder. Bigamy. Secret wife. Hush-hush child. No one in Cottonport wanted to miss the trial of the decade. The gossip had been making the rounds for months, and now the facts would be told for everyone to hear—the whole story laid out in full, or at least enough of it to keep the public entertained for some time to come.

Prominent families were represented in this complicated case. Two members of a wealthy and influential local family, father and son, were in jail and accused of murder. The son had married not one but two women, without benefit of divorce in between, then the first had been murdered. The brother of the victim had married a well-to-do local ranch owner. There were hints that there was more to the whole ordeal than would be covered in this trial. Tantalizing gossip had been drained of every drop of information, and it was time to add more seasoning to the pot.

People around town were saying this was better than any movie show playing at the Roxie Theater, and it was happening right here in town. If a person was lucky enough to get a seat in the courtroom, they would see and hear all the details and be an honored guest at most any dinner or party in town for some time to come, all for being able to relate, firsthand, what the witnesses said and looked like and how the accused reacted.

Lon Grainger had hired a high-powered lawyer from Houston, and the first thing he did was object to the trial happening locally at all. He argued that it should be tried in the county where the murder took place.

"Mr. Dailey," Judge Hodges, also from Houston and quite familiar with the attorney's delaying tactics, said, "we settled this before we came to trial. Although the murder happened in Belton County, the planning and hiring of the individuals involved occurred here. Added to that, Belton County is sparsely populated, the courtroom small, and it would be hard to get a jury together in that venue. The trial will proceed."

When the prosecuting attorney rose to give his opening speech, he was playing to both the jury and the crowded room. He also wanted to acquaint Judge Hodges with all the players in the drama more personally than could be told in dry documents. He told his audience that he was going to tell the story right from the beginning: when and why this unfortunate young woman lost her life, how she was betrayed by the one who swore before God to cherish and protect her, and how that led to her death, plotted and planned by the defendant, who wanted only to promote his own agenda for his son's life, and in doing that, insure connections were made with the local judiciary.

"We won't pull any punches, ladies and gentlemen. The core of the case can be traced right here to Cottonport. We will put blame where blame is due." He strolled up and down in front of the jury box. "And when you have heard the story, when you have been presented with the evidence, you will have no other option other than to find the defendant guilty of arranging for the death of this innocent young woman, and you will learn just how innocent she really was, in the fullest context of the word."

Cardboard fans fluttered all over the courtroom. The windows were open, but the temperatures were hot for early May. Fentress Funeral Home had been passing out the brightly colored, coveted fans, hoping to influence people in the audience assembled outside who were trying to hear the proceedings through the windows to call them the next time there was a death in the family.

When it was the defense attorney's turn, Dailey chose his second chair, Old Man Cyrus Murdock, the oldest lawyer in Cottonport, to make the speech. Bent and hobbling, with white hair flying, and speaking in his homiest vernacular, he said he reckoned it was jealous people trying to do in this pillar of the community, said it was all a misunderstanding. He blamed the people who were trying to take down this law-abiding citizen of being jealous of his success. He aimed to prove it beyond the shadow of a doubt.

When he was composing his opening speech, Dailey had thought to put in something about how honest Lon Grainger was, how well-thought of, but Murdock had cautioned against it. Too many people, he said, had been bamboozled by Lon Grainger at one time or another. It was best not to get folks thinking along those lines. Better to accuse his enemies of jealousy. The Houston lawyer had rethought his plan of making the primary speech. The locals might react better to Murdock than an out-of-towner. He'd do the planning, Murdock the speaking . . . or most of it.

When the two lengthy speeches were complete, the prosecuting attorney called the first witness: the victim's brother, Jonah Aaron Crandall. A few gasps could be heard. They were expressed by the people who weren't well-connected enough to have heard this part of the gossip and didn't know that Dorie Barnett had married the brother of the murdered woman. The judge pounded his gavel. "Quiet in the court! Anyone speaking or making noise of any kind will be ejected from the courtroom! I will not put up with demonstrations of any sort." This trial wasn't going to get away from him. He was known as a no-nonsense judge, and he was determined to live up to his name, even in this circus of a trial.

Dorie gave Jonah's hand a squeeze as his name was called. They had been holding hands during the opening arguments, each gaining comfort in the other's presence. Dorie gave a shuddering sigh as her husband stood and started toward the witness stand. It would be hard on him to have to relate the story of his sister's life and death, and she felt deeply for the pain her husband would endure.

After the swearing in, John Sturgis led Jonah slowly and carefully through the tale of the mentally handicapped young woman and the handsome, wealthy young man who wooed and won her. The defendant's attorney objected a couple of times, but the objections were overruled. Jonah was only stating facts. He said nothing of his own opinion about the subsequent marriage. He didn't even offer an opinion about Letitia's move to the cottage on the edge of one of the wildest, scariest place in Texas, The Big Thicket. He didn't need to. Anyone who wasn't familiar with the daunting region wouldn't have been on the jury. Sturgis had seen to that during jury selection.

Jonah told of using the postmark on Letty's letters to find her when their parents hadn't heard from her and the last letters had spoken of hunger and abandonment.

When the defense attorney questioned him, Jonah never veered from his statements of facts, and he never lost his temper. When asked how he was sure that Letty and Lonnie Grainger were married, he answered, "Because I have their wedding license," and pulled it out of his coat pocket, causing a stir at the defense table.

Dailey kept trying to trip him up, with no success. Finally, the judge said, "Mr. Dailey, move this along. You're going over the same ground."

"No more questions, your honor."

Chapter 42

A short break was declared, and everyone got up to stretch their legs. Dorie excused herself and headed to the ladies' room.

"Married, little brother?" Thomas frowned at Jonah. "Without letting the folks know? What's the story?"

Jonah shrugged. "What's to tell? She's a beautiful woman, and we got married."

Thomas gave a disbelieving frown. "For starters, you've evaded marriage to several beautiful women in the Waco area, so I want to know how she caught you. Where did you meet?"

"On her ranch. She owns the Big B."

Thomas gave a low whistle. "That's a big outfit. I've even heard of it, and I'm not into ranching, at least not since Dad made us work on our spread. Does she own Big B Enterprises, too?"

"Yes, she does."

"They have cotton warehouses up our way, I believe. It's a large business with fingers in a lot of things."

"Yes, it is." He wanted to downplay his marriage. Sooner or later, it would have come to light, but he had hoped it would be later. Still, the whole matter weighed on his mind. The fact that his parents didn't know about it—he hoped they never would, considering the marriage would be over in another couple of months if Dorie insisted on keeping to their bargain—made it certain that his family would not approve of what he had done. Still, he had no regrets, but he didn't want to get into a discussion about it with Thomas, not now, anyway.

"Couldn't you have invited Mom and Dad to the ceremony? Mom is going to be hurt."

"Actually, we eloped. Neither one of us wanted any big, fancy hoopla."

"So you live on her ranch?"

"Yes, but for the period of the trial we are staying here in town. It's too much time and trouble to run back and forth."

In truth, they had discussed the danger involved in being on the road between the Big B and town. Since one attempt had already been made on Jonah's life, it was possible that someone might try again, and Jonah wasn't taking any risks with Dorie and Sarah's lives, either. A suite had been reserved at the Majestic Hotel, and they had moved into it the day before. They had a two-bedroom suite, where Dorie and Sarah shared one room, and Jonah took the other. Crippled Elk drove Annie into town early each morning to care for Sarah while the couple were occupied in the courtroom.

The bailiff and jury returned, putting an end to the conversation, much to Jonah's relief.

"All rise," the bailiff called out. "The court is back in session. The Honorable Elwood Hodges presiding."

The first person called was the county clerk from Marble County. A short, unassuming man, he had been sitting in the back of the courtroom from the beginning. After being sworn in, Sturgis asked, "Mr. Jeeves, have you had a chance to study the marriage license that had been issued to Lon Grainger, Junior and Letitia Crandall."

"I have," he answered.

"In your opinion, is it an authentic marriage license?"

"It is."

"In your opinion, is there any way it could be a forgery? A fake marriage license?"

"No, sir. It looks like the licenses we issue. I would swear it is authentic."

"You *are* swearing that, sir." Sturgis smiled. "And is that your signature at the bottom."

Jeeves pulled the document closer to his face and studied it. "Yes. It is definitely my signature."

A few minutes later, Dailey tried to shake his testimony, but the little man was like a bulldog, holding fast to his sworn statement that the paper was authentic and legal.

The next person called was Thomas Elijah Crandall. Jonah and Dorie looked questioningly at each other. Neither had known why Sturgis had sent for him, but that fact became obvious as the testimony proceeded.

Thomas was sworn in, and Sturgis asked him what his profession was. "I guess you could say I have several," he answered. "I am a vice president in my father's bank, but here lately I have been spending most of my time and energy in the airline industry."

"You own an airline, Mr. Crandall?"

"I own stock in several, but I am most interested in a smaller, local airline that I own. It operates here in Texas. I own hangars and rent out space in various towns. I rent airplanes. I buy and sell airplanes. I'm pretty much interested in anything that flies, you might say. It's my passion."

Sturgis then asked about the makeup of the Crandall family and led him through Letty's early years, reinforcing Jonah's account of their sister and her disability. The story proceeded to the courtship of Letitia and Lonnie, her parents' objections, and the elopement. Thomas' testimony backed up everything Jonah had told the court. When the defense attorney took over, one of the first questions he asked was whether Thomas and Jonah had discussed what they were going to say.

"No, Mr. Dailey. I haven't seen nor spoken to my brother for well over a year, and he didn't know I was going to be here today until I showed up. We haven't discussed this matter at all."

The questions were short and quick after that, and Thomas was dismissed.

"Your Honor"—Sturgis approached the bench—"the next witness I'm going to call is the sheriff of the county where the murder took place. I anticipate that it will take some time for my questioning, and also for the defense. Maybe I suggest that we recess until after lunch?"

"That's a good idea, Mr. Sturgis. Court is in recess until 1:30."

"All rise," the bailiff called out.

A small group was gathered around the table in the conference room. Lunch had been brought in, ordered by the prosecutor's office for the benefit of the witnesses who had been called from various locations around the state. Jonah was included in the gathering, due to the fear that still hung over him concerning the earlier threats. Sturgis wasn't taking any unnecessary chances with his witnesses. He said he had a feeling there was more involved in these matters than just Letitia Crandall Grainger's death.

The prosecuting attorney had warned the audience that the afternoon's testimony might be graphic and the ladies might not want to be present. This word spread, causing the size of the crowd that wanted to get favored seats in the courtroom to grow exponentially. A few had hastily grabbed a bite to eat and hurried back to stand in the hall, ready to be the first ones through the doors when they were unlocked.

Dorie had gone back to the hotel. Still emotionally fragile after the birth and death of her daughter, she didn't think she could bear hearing the gruesome testimony that was to come next. The proceedings so far had been tiring, even though she was only there to listen and observe. Jonah urged her to skip the afternoon session and take a nap. She agreed that it would be the best thing.

"And while I'm there, why don't I make arrangements to have dinner served in the parlor of our suite? You can invite your brother to eat with us. I'm sure he is anxious to see Sarah. Is there anything he doesn't eat?"

"Not a thing, as you can tell from looking at him," Jonah joked. He squeezed her arm as she left him to join the deputy who was to accompany her to the Majestic Hotel. Before he let go, he quickly leaned toward her and kissed her gently on the lips.

The surprise kiss flustered her, and she felt her cheeks warm. Touching her hand to her face, she smiled at him and turned away, wondering if the show of affection was for the audience in the crowded hallway or if it was real.

The group that had gathered in the conference room had been cautioned not to discuss the trial or anything that pertained to it, so the conversation was limited to the weather, the highways, the continuing depression, and Thomas's favorite subject—airplanes and flying.

"You ain't gonna get me in one o' them things," the Belton County Sheriff proclaimed. "If God had wanted us to fly, we'd been borned with wings."

"Air travel is here, Sheriff," Thomas said. "Even if you never fly, your children and grandchildren will live in a world where it is commonplace."

"I must admit," the Marble County clerk nervously admitted, "I'd like to try it sometime. It must be very interesting to see the earth from high up like that."

"You come on up to Waco, Mr. Jeeves, and I'll give you a spin."

"It sounds like you have really expanded your business since I last saw you," Jonah said.

"Yes, I have, and I'd like to tell you about it. I imagine you have things you can tell me, too," Thomas replied, eyebrows raised.

"I'm supposed to invite you to eat with us tonight."

"So?"

Jonah continued eating in silence, and Thomas followed suit, until the sheriff and the clerk finished their meal and left. "I didn't want to talk while there was anyone in the room except us," Jonah explained.

"You sure are being hush-hush, little brother."

"Yes, I am, and I'll tell you all about it tonight."

"Tell me where and when, and I'll be there."

Jonah told him the suite number. "Dorie is having the meal delivered to the suite so we can talk in private. You'll understand when you've heard everything that has been going on. Come about six o'clock."

"I can't wait," Thomas replied.

Chapter 43

The testimony of Sheriff Cooley of Belton County took all afternoon, as foreseen by Sturgis. He told how the neighbors of the murdered woman, the Swifts, had come to his office to report Letitia Grainger missing and how the victim's brother showed up the next day.

"They hadn't heard from her in a while and went over to her house, and there was that poor little girl . . ."

"Objection!"

"Just tell what happened, Sheriff, without comment, if you please."

"Yessir, that's what I was doin'. That there little girl was all by herself, and she was scared and hungry. She said her mama done went into the woods to find 'em some berries and plums and stuff to eat, on account o' they's done run outta food and money, on account of her papa hadn't sent 'em any money to buy food with."

"Objection!"

"Just tell what the girl said, Sheriff."

"That's what I'm doin'! That's what the girl said."

"Continue," Judge Hodges said, "but only tell what you actually saw or heard, Sheriff."

"That's what I'm doin', Judge."

The testimony continued for some time. Sheriff Cooley related that it was late afternoon by the time the Swifts had finished telling him about finding Sarah alone in the house and taking her back home with them to feed her and keep her safe. He had heard Sarah's story firsthand from the child herself, who was upset and worried about her mother.

"It was might near dark by then, and the Swifts needed to get back home, so I decided to wait until morning to go to the victim's house, 'cause I sure wasn't goin' in The Thicket in the dark. 'Course, I didn't know she was a victim then, not 'til the next day.

"Next morning, first thing, Mr. Crandall showed up, looking for his sister. He'd done been to the post office and found out it were the Swifts who mailed the letters his sister sent home to her family, and he came to get me to go with him to investigate, and mostly to show him the way to his sister's place and the Swifts' place. I had to tell him about his poor . . . er, his little niece bein' found all by herself and all."

Sturgis led him through the venture into The Big Thicket looking for Letty and the discovery of her body.

"And did you determine the cause of death, Sheriff?"

"I did."

"And it was?"

"A bullet to the head. Or maybe the one to the heart. Either one coulda done the job."

The courtroom erupted into excited chatter.

The judge's gavel rang. "Order in the court." Bang! Bang! "There will be silence or I will have the courtroom cleared of all observers!"

When it was the defense attorney's turn, his questions took a more gruesome turn when he asked if the wild animals had damaged the body.

"Yessir, they did."

The sheriff was led into a protracted account, until the judge had enough and said, "We get the picture. Move it along, counselor."

"Yes, Your Honor. Sheriff, isn't it possible the victim was killed by a wild animal, a bear, say, or a panther, since both are numerous in The Big Thicket?"

"No, sir, I wouldn't say that."

"Why? Why wouldn't you?"

"On account, why would somebody come along an' put bullets into a body what was already dead?"

Again, the room burst into talk, and Judge Hodges rapped his gavel.

Dailey didn't give up. "Sheriff, isn't it possible that someone came along and found a woman gravely hurt and suffering and decided to put her out of her misery?"

"Objection!" rang out, but before the judge could rule, Sheriff Cooley got in his opinion.

"That's the stupidest thing I ever did hear. You might do that in the big city of Houston, but down in Belton County, if we find someone done mauled by a bear or a panther, we take 'em to the doctor to try to save 'em."

There was no saving the decorum at that point, no matter how much Judge Hodges rapped.

"Court is adjourned until nine o'clock in the morning."

Chapter 44

Talk around the dinner tables in the county was anything but pleasant that evening, except in the Crandall suite at the hotel. Jonah and Thomas had agreed that none of the day's testimony would be repeated in front of Dorie or Sarah. It wasn't that Dorie didn't know what had happened to Letty, but he thought she didn't need to hear the gruesome details.

Delighted to see his niece for the first time in several years, Thomas squatted in front of her. "My goodness, you've grown!" She looked at him dubiously. "Do you remember your Uncle Thomas?" Jonah asked. She shook her head.

"Don't you remember the time I took you on the back of a horse with me and we walked all around the yard at your grandparents' house?"

"That was you? I remember that! It was fun."

"Yes. That was me."

"And Mama kept calling, 'Don't let her fall off.'"

"Yes. That's right."

That event unleashed a flood of memories, and Sarah began to recall other things about the time at her grandparents, and she and Thomas visited until time to eat dinner. Jonah listened to the stories and added some of his own of happy times when the family was all together.

Dorie and Annie had set a fine table with the hotel's china and silver, and Dorie had ordered the food early in the day to be ready at six o'clock. She sent Annie to the flower shop for an arrangement to adorn the table, and all was in preparation when Jonah and Thomas arrived after the day's courtroom proceedings.

Annie stayed long enough to meet Thomas then left to meet Crippled Elk and drive back to the Big B. "I'll see you in the morning," she told Sarah.

"Annie calls me Usdi Tsisqua," she told Thomas. "That means Little Bird."

"That is a good name for you," her uncle agreed.

"She says I hide in the bushes and listen and learn, and she says someday I'll fly like a bird."

"I can make the flying part happen. I'll take you flying in an airplane."

"You can fly in an areoplane?"

"An air-plane," he corrected. "Yes. I own an airplane. I'll take you flying."

Dorie started asking questions about the various related businesses he was involved in, and before they knew it, the entire mealtime had been spent talking about things far removed from the trial and the terrible events that had led up to it.

When Sarah began to nod off, Dorie said, "It's time for Little Bird to go to bed." She pushed her chair back and reached for the sleepy child.

"I want to hear more about areo . . . airplanes," Sarah protested.

"I'll still be here tomorrow, Little Bird," Thomas said. "I promise we'll have time to talk more."

When Dorie closed the door between the parlor and bedroom, Jonah sighed. "We got through that OK. I didn't want any of the details of Letty's death to come up."

"Poor kid. She went through a lot. More than I heard about today, I imagine."

"You're right about that. Sturgis is going to call on her to testify."

"You're kidding!"

"No, I'm not. He said everyone needs to hear firsthand what she went through so Grainger doesn't get away with it."

"But isn't that putting her through a lot?"

"Maybe, but she's gotten over it for the most part, and it's important that Grainger is punished for what he did."

"I agree with that." The men got up from the table and moved to the sofa and chairs. "But I hate it that all those memories will be brought back to her." They took comfortable seats. "Now, little brother, tell me more about this marriage and the rest of the story about what is going on."

Jonah realized that he was going to have to tell his brother more about what had occurred, especially since it was tied to Grainger, too, even though not directly connected with Letty's death. He only hoped he could do it in such a way as to not invade too much on Dorie's privacy.

"Start with how you ended up here," Thomas said.

Jonah leaned forward and rested his elbows on his knees. "When Lonnie Grainger first showed up at the bank to do business with Father, he was asking questions about buying into a local company, and he filled out some papers concerning Grainger Industries. I got into the file before I left, looking for where he might have taken Letty, and I saw the Graingers were both from Cottonport. I didn't come here first, though. I went to where the postmark led me. Today you heard about what I found when I got there. Letty had been buried there in the churchyard, and I took Sarah with me. I didn't know if anyone would be looking for her or not. I couldn't figure out why they didn't kill her, too, if they knew about her."

He slumped in his chair. "I knew from the beginning Grainger had something to do with Letty's death. No one else would have a reason to do it. No one else would know where she was. It had to have something to do with the marriage, and that put Sarah at risk. I stashed her in a place I thought she would be safe from anyone looking for her. That turned out to be a big mistake."

"You didn't take her to the folks because . . .?"

"Because that's the first place anyone would look, and Lonnie Grainger would have claim on her as his daughter."

"Stop right there. Do I understand there is a Lon Grainger and a Lonnie Grainger?"

"Right. Senior and Junior, respectively. No respect intended."

Thomas chuckled. "Of course not, and it's Lon Senior on trial today, not Lonnie?"

"Right."

"OK. Continue."

"I came here to Cottonport. Met Dorie, who was having her own problems with Grainger, Senior."

"Oh?"

"You see, he owns land adjoining hers, and Navco Oil drilled test wells on his property and hit pay dirt, but they told him the main field is on Big B land."

"I can guess what comes next. He tried to talk her out of the Big B."

"In a way. When she wouldn't think of selling, he decided the way to get what he wanted was to marry her."

Thomas gave a low whistle. "That's one way, I guess. And she wasn't interested in marrying him?"

"No. No way would she marry him." Jonah had no intention of telling his brother about Dorie offering him the marriage bargain. No way would he tell Thomas about the rape or Dorie's pregnancy. "So when you asked me about why we eloped instead of taking our time and having a proper formal ceremony—the kind Mom would have wanted to see—it was because it saved a lot of hassle just to do it. Otherwise . . ." Otherwise he would be dead before he and Dorie could marry.

"Did that stop him?"

"Not a bit. Grainger decided he could marry a widow just as well."

Thomas stared at his brother. "He tried to kill you?"

"Tried to have me killed."

"How?"

"First was a bullet through the front window."

"He missed, I take it."

"Yes. I leaned over to see something Sarah wanted to show me just as the gunman fired."

"I almost forgot Sarah was in this."

"When Dorie and I married, I retrieved her and brought her to the Big B to live."

"She seems like she likes it with you two."

"She does." He'd leave talk about adopting her until later. "But she had another harrowing event happen to her."

"Poor kid! What happened?"

"After the bullet missed me, Dorie was insistent I stay close to home and out of range of gunmen. When they couldn't get a good bead on me, they decided to get me out where they could reach me."

"Just how did they plan to do that?"

"They kidnapped Sarah."

"What?" Thomas leaned forward and looked hard at Jonah. "Was she hurt?"

"No, she wasn't. The man who took her pretended to be a deliveryman. He put a chloroform rag over her nose, and she went to sleep. He took off in a van, knowing that I would follow."

"And you did, I take it."

"Not before Dorie did."

"Dorie?"

"She jumped in my old truck and took off. By the time I got out the door, she was gone, and I had to go in the barn and get her car to follow."

"Did you catch up?"

"Yes, but not before . . ." He paused, rubbing his hands over his eyes. He could still see the scene in his memory.

"Before?"

"They thought it was me in my truck. Dorie was wearing overalls and a man's winter coat. They thought it was me . . ." He still lost his breath thinking about what had happened—what might have happened. He took a shuddering gasp. "Another truck pulled in beside her and rammed my truck, sent it rolling over and over until it landed in the Brazos."

"My God!"

"It was upside down. Crippled Elk—he works at the Big B—came along, and we got her out before it sank."

"Thank God she was safe."

"Yes, but . . ."

"But what?"

"She was pregnant."

Thomas sat back, waiting to hear the outcome.

"The baby was born the next day. It wasn't big enough to survive."

Thomas put his hand on Jonah's arm. "I'm so sorry. So very sorry."

"Dorie named her Dawn, because she was born at daybreak."

They sat, unspeaking, until Dorie made her presence known. They both jumped when she spoke. They hadn't realized she was standing in the door, listening.

"It was Dawn's funeral that brought all this to a head. It was Sarah who did it." She came to the sofa and sat down next to Jonah. He took her hand and held it between both of his. Tears were flowing down her cheeks. "You tell the rest," she said in a choked voice.

"We weren't expecting many folks at the funeral," he said, "but the church was full. Everyone stood up to go out to the churchyard for the interment, and Sarah spotted Lonnie. She stood up before God and man, as the saying goes, and announced that he was her father and had left them alone and hungry."

"Good for her!" Thomas said.

"That's when it all came out. Lonnie said he thought his father had gotten him a divorce and paid Letty money to support her and Sarah in style. Lon Senior thought they were dead. Lonnie's pregnant wife was there, along with her parents, the local judge, and his wife."

"Wife?" Thomas echoed.

"Well, she thought she was," Dorie said. "There for a while."

"There was a big hullabaloo in the church, with everyone yelling."

"Are we going to hear all this in court?"

"I imagine we are going to hear the part about the funeral, but not about the attempts made on my life," Jonah said.

"Why not that part?"

"Because we don't have any proof, at this point, that Grainger had anything to do with the gunshot or the truck being pushed into the river."

"Then we have to get proof."

"Yes, but let's get Letty's death taken care of first."

"And how are they going to prove Grainger had anything to do with that?"

"Lonnie Junior is going to testify against him in order to save his own skin."

"Let Lonnie off free? After what he did to Letty?" He stood and pounded his fist into his other palm. "No way is that going to happen!"

"No. Not free, but he won't be tried for murder. He swears he would never have had Letty killed and didn't know it's what his father had planned. He's still in trouble for bigamy. He sure knew he was already married when he married the judge's daughter. He just hadn't fessed up to it yet, and when he told his father that he was already married, he thought his father was going to get him a divorce and sweep it all under the rug."

"Grainger didn't actually do the killing himself, did he?"

"No. He hired two men to do it for him."

"But no one saw them, did they? So how can they be caught?"

"Oh, someone saw them, but they don't know it."

"Who? Who saw them?"

"Sarah."

Chapter 45

The crowd grew each day. Even the area near the windows was being staked out by people trying to hear the testimony. The news had leaked out that Lonnie Grainger, or "Junior," the crowd called him, was going to testify, and people were lined up inside and out to get a chance to get the story firsthand. Talk was that he was turning against his father. "Brave," one man was heard saying, "biting the hand that feeds you."

"Think like a Grainger," his companion said. "If his old man goes to the chair, who inherits? Junior, that's who. Maybe he's smarter than people give him credit for."

The rumors were correct, and Lon Grainger, Junior, swore "to tell the truth, the whole truth, and nothing but the truth," and people hung on his every word. Question by question, Sturgis led him through the story of how one summer day a few years ago his father sent him to a bank in Waco to explore the possibilities of buying into a business in that area. While visiting with the president of the bank, Aaron Crandall, he was presented with the loveliest young woman he had ever met: Letitia, the daughter of said President Crandall.

He lost his heart. Fell in love with her sweetness, simplicity, beauty. Her parents tried to scare him off, told him all sorts of things. Told him she was simple, that she'd never be able to run a household by herself. Told him she'd always have to be protected more than most women. He could see for himself that she was guileless and unassuming. That's what made her special, not like all the other women he had known. That's why he loved her, really loved her, not like the girls he had been smitten with in the past.

So they ran away and got married. If he had to provide help in the home for the rest of her life, then so be it. He was from a wealthy family. He could afford it. After a couple of weeks, they went back and told her family what they had done. The family was not pleased.

By then it had occurred to him that he needed to be very careful when he presented this development to his father, who had always stressed the importance of marrying well. Lon Senior had taken his own advice—the second time, that is. Lonnie's mother had no money, nor did her family have any influence, but she died when Lonnie was small, and Lon remarried an heiress.

So Lonnie went back to Cottonport and told his father about the wonderful girl he had met. He left out the part about getting married. He had hoped to build up to that. After days of vigorous debates and arguments, Lon had finally said, "If she's so special, keep her on the side where nobody will know, but for heaven's sake, don't marry her." It was already too late for that advice.

By the time Lonnie went back to his wife, it quickly became obvious that she was pregnant, and he realized he had a problem. She couldn't live alone, and he couldn't live with her. He tried to get the marriage license, which the minister had handed to Letitia after the ceremony, but he couldn't figure out what she had done with it. Her mother was beside herself with worry over Letty's condition, so it was worked out that she would remain at home with her parents, since Lonnie "spent all his time traveling for his father." He would visit any time he could.

Over the next few months, Lonnie realized it was not working out as he had hoped, so he did what he had always done: ignored the problem. Sarah was born, a beautiful child, adored by her grandparents, which made it easier to let everything float along as it had been. Time sped by, with Lonnie showing up every few months with money and presents and plenty of charm. It was enough . . . until it wasn't.

Lonnie had no clue as to why Letty's father got on such a tear about him being a man and caring for his own wife and child, but there it was. He had to do something. Since Lon Senior had no clue that Letty was still in his life, much less that he was actually married to her, he couldn't go to his father for help.

"So what did you do?" Sturgis asked, using a kindly tone of voice, full of sympathy for the young man before him— poor young man who had gotten himself into such a jam.

"I bought her a house. A nice little house. Not a mansion, but one any woman ought to be proud of having."

"And where was this house?"

"Down in Belton County."

"Belton County, huh? Mighty rural area, isn't it?"

"I guess so. Letty was real taken with the wildflowers."

"Did you move her there?"

"Yes."

"And your little girl? Sarah?"

"Yes."

"That's close to The Big Thicket, isn't it?"

"Yes. That's right."

"And you do know what The Big Thicket is, don't you?"

"Yes. It's a scary place . . . wild. But the house wasn't in The Big Thicket."

"Just close to it."

"That's right."

"And you thought this woman, this simple woman whom you had been cautioned could not care for herself, could manage a house and child by herself?" Sturgis' voice had lost the sympathetic tone it had once shown, becoming more strident with each question.

"Well, you see, I thought maybe I could find somebody

to come by every day and help out."

"Did you find someone like that?"

Lonnie hung his head. "No, sir." He looked up. "But I did find a couple not too far away who agreed to come by and check on Letty and Sarah from time to time. I paid them to do that, and to fetch groceries and stuff they needed from town."

Sturgis voice regained its fatherly tone. "And you checked on them yourself? At least in the beginning?"

"Oh, yessir! I went every month and took food and money and presents."

"Tell me, what made you choose a place so far away from others to buy your wife and child a home?" He asked it kindly and turned away as he did.

Lonnie dropped his head once again, having come to the realization that his motive might not be in keeping with what most people thought a husband ought to do.

"I thought it was best that Letty not be around people she might tell her story to, people who might know my family." He actually sounded ashamed.

"So word wouldn't get back to your father?"

"Yessir," he mumbled.

Sturgis walked away from the witness chair, distancing himself before he asked the next question.

"But there came a time, didn't it, when you had to tell your father?"

"Yes."

"Why?"

"Well, he had it all worked out that I should marry Myrnalee Blackmon. I had to tell him I was already married."

"Myrnalee Blackmon. That's Judge Blackmon's daughter, isn't it?"

A ripple of voices went through the courtroom. "Quiet in the court." Judge Hodges banged his gavel.

"Did you tell him right off? Before you married Myrnalee?"

"No, sir."

"You already went through a wedding ceremony with Myrnalee before you told him you were married to Letitia?"

"Yessir."

"How long had you been married to Myrnalee when you told him?"

"Almost a year."

"Almost a year, huh? For almost a year you had two wives." He shook his head as he walked away. "What did your father say when you told him?"

"He was angry at me."

"Very angry?"

"Yes. Very angry."

"But he calmed down? He agreed to help you?" He turned and looked at Lonnie.

"Yes. He said he'd take care of it. He said he'd see that I got a divorce and that Letty wouldn't be a problem then."

"That's what he said? She wouldn't be a problem?"

"Yes. I told him I wanted her to have the house and plenty of money to live on. If he thought she needed to live someplace else, someplace she wouldn't be traced back to me, that was OK, but I wanted her well taken care of."

"And did he say she would be?"

"Yes, he did." Sturgis stared at Lonnie until the younger man understood what was being implied by what he had just said. "But I didn't mean have her killed! I didn't! I never wanted Letty harmed in any way!"

"It didn't work out that way, did it?"

"Objection, Your Honor!" Dailey yelled.

There was a short break, then it was the defense's turn. It didn't take long, probably because the more Lonnie tried to explain, the worse it sounded. His proclamations of love and caring for his wife notwithstanding, he came across as a spoiled rich kid who was used to having his way and being backed up by an indulging father. Dailey tried to get Lonnie to say that he was the one who arranged to have Letty killed, but the hapless husband wouldn't budge from his story. Dailey finally figured out that the more questions he asked, the worse it was for his client. "No more questions, Your Honor," closed the morning session.

The hoard observing the trial from both inside and outside the courtroom had plenty to talk about over the lunch hour, but it was quiet in the conference room where the witnesses, sans Lonnie, were eating the sandwiches brought in from the Main Street Deli. The prosecuting attorney and the sheriff, still cautious about the safety of not only witnesses, but anyone connected to the whole ordeal, weren't taking any chances. Keeping the players close at hand was insurance that they would stay safe. The sheriff also had plenty of armed deputies in the building, both in the hallways and inside the courtroom, standing against the walls, watching the observers. It was better to be overly cautious. Lon Grainger was an arrogant braggart who had been saying that he'd never be convicted. There was no telling what reaction might come, whether he was found innocent or guilty.

The list of witnesses was fairly public. The morning witness had been entered as "L. Grainger, Jr." The afternoon started with S. Grainger. People were buzzing about who that might be. When S. Grainger was called, the bailiff said, "The witness is being brought into the court, Your Honor," and walked to the side door. Judge Hodges rapped his gavel, and the crowd quieted. After a minute, the door swung open, and Annie appeared, holding Sarah's hand.

Sturgis walked over to Sarah and leaned down. "Are you ready, Sarah?"

"Little Bird, she is brave. She will do fine," Annie answered for her.

Sturgis extended his hand, and Sarah released Annie's to take his. "Annie, you may sit where she can see you." He looked at Sarah. "She'll be right there"—he pointed toward the row of seats where Jonah and Dorie sat—"and when you are through, she will take you back. OK?" Sarah nodded.

He walked her to the witness chair that sat to the right and slightly lower than Judge Hodges' seat. The judge smiled at her. "Now, don't you be frightened. I have a granddaughter about your age, and she'd tell you I'm not scary at all, even if I do have this black robe on. It's just something judges wear."

The court clerk approached Sarah. Judge Hodges said, "Tell us nice and loud what your full name is."

"Sarah Ann Grainger."

The clerk extended the Bible in her hand. "Do you swear to tell the truth, the whole truth, and nothing but the truth, so help you God?" Sarah looked puzzled.

"Do you promise to tell the truth today in court?" Hodges asked.

"I always tell the truth," Sarah said. "My mama said it's important to never lie." A murmur ran through the courtroom. Judge Hodges lifted his gavel but thought better of it and put it back down.

Sturgis was walking a thin line in questioning Sarah. On the one hand, he wanted the judge and jury to see her vulnerability and the suffering she had endured and to realize how the loss of her mother would impact her life. On the other hand, he didn't want Sarah to get so upset she would start crying or lose control of her emotions. He had talked to her in private and thought he had an idea of how strong she was, but one could never be sure of a small child, especially in new surroundings.

He led her through her memories of living in the house by the edge of the woods, and he asked her about her father coming to visit them. He even had her point out her father, who was sitting on the defense side of the courtroom.

"He's right there," Sarah pointed out. "But I don't want him to be my father any more. I told him that. I want Uncle Jonah to be my father."

"Objection!" Dailey was quick on his feet.

"Mr. Dailey, we are dealing with a child here," Judge Hodges said, "A child who has been through a very traumatic time. I'm going to allow some leniency with this testimony. If we start telling her what she can and can't say, we may miss something important. The only person who is to interrupt Sarah's testimony is me." He turned toward her. "You go ahead, Sarah. You say anything you want to."

Sarah nodded her head. "I saw him at the church that day, and I told him I didn't want him to be my father any more. A father is supposed to take care of his little girl, Mama said so, and he didn't take care of me and Mama. We were hungry, and he didn't come and bring us any food or money."

Dorie heard sniffles behind her. She had her own hankie out to catch the tears that escaped and rolled down her cheeks. When she turned, she saw other women wiping their eyes.

"And so what did your mama do?" Sturgis asked. "When you ran out of food, what did she do?"

"She went into the woods to find us some berries to eat. She said they were good. She took a bucket to put them in."

"What did she tell you before she left?"

"She said she'd be back."

"What else did she tell you?"

"She said to hide if anyone came while she was gone."

"And did anyone come?"

"Yes. Two men came."

"And did you hide?"

"Yes. When I heard the truck coming, I went out the back door and hid behind the wood pile."

"Did you stay there?"

"No, sir. When those men were in the house, I sneaked up to the window and looked."

"What were they doing?"

"I think maybe they were looking for something. They took everything out of the shelves and threw it on the floor, and they took the pictures off the wall." She gave a big sigh. "They made an awful mess."

"How many men were there?"

"Two."

"Can you tell us what they looked like?"

She gave a shrug. "Just men."

"Were they both the same size?"

"No. One was smaller."

"Shorter?"

"Shorter, and thinner, too."

"Was his skin light, like you and me? Or dark, like Annie's?"

"It was light. Both of them, their skin was light."

"What were they wearing? Could you tell?"

"The littler man, he was dressed like the men who work on Miss Dorie's ranch."

"Like the men who work on the Big B?"

"Yes. But not the other man."

"The second man, he was taller?"

"Yes, and he was wearing a brown shirt and pants, like the men over there." She waved toward the wall near her, where two deputies stood.

"How tall was he? As tall as, say, your Uncle Jonah? Taller?"

Sarah gazed around the courtroom. "He was about . . ." Her eyes lit up. "There he is! There's the man." She pointed toward a deputy standing against the wall in the back of the room.

"Sarah," Judge Hodges said, "That man works here. He wouldn't . . ." He stopped speaking when he saw that the person Sarah had pointed out was moving toward the door.

"Somebody stop that man!" he commanded.

With that, the deputy pulled his gun from the holster. Taking aim at Sarah, he pulled the trigger.

Chapter 46

Pandemonium broke out all over the courtroom. Women were screaming. Many people jumped out of their seats and rushed into the aisles, making it difficult for the deputies on the sides of the room to get to the shooter. Sturgis was looking toward where Sarah was pointing and saw the deputy draw his gun. He threw himself in front of Sarah just in time to be struck by the bullet meant for her.

Jonah vaulted over the railing that separated the observers from the participants in the front of the room. Dorie would have been right behind him, but she couldn't climb over the barrier in the dress she was wearing. They were both screaming, "Sarah! Sarah!" Annie closed her eyes and appeared to be in prayer.

As the deputies who had been standing on the left side of the room reached the shooter and grabbed for his arm, he took aim at Lon Grainger and fired. Lon, having stood up to face the accused murderer and yell, "You fool!" made a perfect target. The bullet went right through his chest.

Sarah appeared to be unaffected, other than the fact that her eyes were open wide as she observed everything going on around her. Jonah reached her first, with Dorie close behind. Sarah's arms wrapped around him as he picked her up and they hurried through the side door to the courtroom, Dorie and Judge Hodges close behind.

The judge later ordered the proceedings to be declared a mistrial. It was not necessary to reschedule. The defendant was dead.

John Sturgis had been shot in the shoulder. Although painful, the wound was not life threatening. The shooter, Carl Bodkin, was a deputy who had been on the job for three years. He admitted to being paid by Lon Grainger, Senior, to kill Letitia. He knew nothing about Sarah's existence as Letty's daughter until she testified.

He also confessed to being the person behind the attacks on Jonah, which also had been ordered and paid for by Lon Senior. In order to avoid the death penalty, he freely gave information pertaining to all crimes, pled guilty to shooting Letty, kidnapping Sarah, and attempting to kill Jonah. When he planned Sarah's kidnapping, he had thought she was Jonah's child. He took her to lure Jonah away from the Big B.

There was no trial for Bodkin. Judge Hodges, who stayed long enough to preside over the hearings, sentenced him to life in prison with no chance of parole. The other man, Pete, who had worked on the Big B Ranch and funneled information back to the deputy, had left Texas for good.

Thomas went back to Waco, left with the difficult job of telling his parents how their daughter had died. Jonah assured him that he would return home as soon as possible and bring Sarah with him.

"And your wife, too, little brother?" he asked. "They'll want to meet her."

"We'll see." Jonah tried to avoid a promise. He was only too aware that the marriage bargain only had a few weeks left, and he was going to use every day of it trying to make the deal a permanent one.

"Uncle Jonah, when are you going to buy a car?" Sarah asked a couple of days later. "Since your truck got crashed, you don't have anything to drive if you want to go to town."

"I guess I'd better see to that, hadn't I, Punkin?"

"Yes. I think you need to buy one like Miss Dorie's." She glanced at Dorie to see how she reacted to that suggestion.

"I don't know about that. I think I'd like to get another truck."

"But I like to ride in Miss Dorie's car better than your truck."

He smiled at Dorie, who was looking very serious.

"If you get a car, maybe we could go to town sometimes." Sarah had become fascinated with town since having stayed at the hotel for several days. She had spent a lot of time looking out the fourth floor window at the hotel, observing all the storefronts and the people going up and down the street. It was very different from her home near The Big Thicket, and she was ready to see all that town had to offer.

"We could go to town in a truck."

"No, Uncle Jonah. It would be more fun to go in a car like Miss Dorie's, and she doesn't like anyone else to drive her car, so you need to get one for yourself."

"Let me get these dishes washed, then I'm going to mix up some cookies. You want to help with cookies, Little Bird? Or you want to talk about cars?"

Sarah slid out of her chair. "I want to make cookies, Annie. I can talk to Uncle Jonah about buying a car later."

As they left the kitchen, Dorie said, "Jonah, come to the office with me, please. We need to talk about something."

They settled themselves in what at one time had been their usual seats—she behind the desk and he in front. *This feels like the first time I came in here,* Jonah thought. *The day she proposed marriage to me.*

"I want to buy you a vehicle," she said. "A truck or car, whichever you want."

He stared at her. "I'm not going to take a vehicle from you."

"That was part of our original deal, that I'd buy you a car."

"No. You said you'd buy one. I didn't accept."

"You agreed to marry me."

"Yes, but I didn't agree to take a car."

She sighed. "It is because of me that your truck is gone."

"No. It is because of Grainger that my truck is gone."

"And he was trying to kill you because of me. I owe you a truck."

"I will not, under any circumstances, take a vehicle, either car or truck, from you."

"You are breaking our agreement."

"When you offered, you thought I was broke, a cowboy living on what I could earn mending fences and hustling cows. You know better now. I can buy any car I want. Money is no object."

Dorie was silent as she pondered his words. It was true that she thought she had married a penniless cowpoke. The fact that he came from a wealthy family explained how he seemed to have more social knowledge than he let on. It had puzzled her early on. It was like he had been pretending to not know about things like luxury hotels, tips, and fine dining, when all the time he had acted with sophistication and manners denoting a fine upbringing.

Dorie thought she was avoiding a problem when she suggested the loveless marriage. Now, she realized, she had initiated a whole new one. Her father's teachings came back, as they often did when she had something difficult to solve. *"Face it dead-on." That's what Big B would say. "Face it and get it over with. It's not fixin' to go away. It'll only get grow and get worse."*

"You know there are only about six weeks left in our bargain, don't you?" She kept her face schooled and her emotions in check, even though she felt like breaking into tears at the thought.

"Yes. I know."

"I went into this because of the threat from Grainger. Now that he's dead, we can end this agreement now."

"Are you breaking the bargain?"

"The reason for the bargain is moot."

"So you want . . .?"

"I'm saying we can divorce now."

"And break the bargain that I went into in all good faith?" He raised his eyebrows.

"It wouldn't be breaking it if we both agree."

"And if I don't?"

She was silent, playing with a scrap of paper in her hands as she had done that first day.

"You owe me these last weeks." His voice was stern.

"It's not like you couldn't find another place to live. You're going to go back to Waco anyway."

"You owe me," he repeated. "You owe me almost six more weeks."

"What does it matter, these last days of a marriage that isn't a marriage?"

He stood and walked to the back of the desk. "What matters," he said, "is that I'm going to persuade you to make it a real marriage. A forever marriage."

She stood and put out her hands to block him from coming too close. "You promised me. You knew it wasn't going to be . . ."

"I didn't promise a thing about not kissing you."

He put his arms around her and pulled her close, so close they fit from lips to toes, each melding into the other's body. He looked deep into her eyes and pressed his lips on hers.

She never dreamed a kiss could be soul-stirring, as if it was sealing them together forever.

When he finally released her, he stepped back and said, "We'll talk more about it later."

Chapter 47

"You want to go to town and pick out something to ride in, Punkin?" he asked Sarah a few days later. "Or do you want to stay here with Annie?"

Her eyes lit up. "I want to go buy a car. Can I, Annie?"

"I think I can manage by myself, Usdi Tsisqua. You go help uncle buy car."

Jonah grinned. "Let's go upstairs and put on going-to-town clothes. Annie, we'll eat lunch in town."

"You make that girl very happy. She been wanting to go to town. She wants to see what's in all those stores and what all those people are doing. She'd never seen so many people as when we were in town for the trial. She was curious about everybody and everything."

Jonah dressed in a suit and tie, and Sarah put on her favorite purple plaid dress.

"Are we going to take Miss Dorie's car?"

"No, Punkin. We'll take her truck. She doesn't mind if I drive that."

"Are you going to buy one like hers?"

"Probably not, but I'll buy something nice. We'll look around when we get to town."

Their first stop was the bank. "I'd like to speak with someone about setting up a new account," he told the young man at the teller's window.

"Yes, sir, Mr. Crandall." The teller knew who Jonah was. Since the famous trial and shoot-out, everyone in town did. "That would be Mister Hewlett. That's his desk back there on the right."

Jonah took Sarah by the hand and approached the big, mahogany desk set apart from the others. Hewlett, too, recognized him immediately. "Good day, Mr. Crandall. Welcome to Citizens Bank. How can I help you?"

"I'd like to open an account here. I'll be buying a vehicle today, and I need to transfer money from my bank in Waco so as to have funds locally."

"Certainly, sir. Certainly. Have a seat."

Jonah proceeded to give the name of his Waco bank and filled out several forms. The amount of money he wished to transfer made Mr. Hewlett blink a couple of times, but he didn't embarrass himself by whistling. He was a banker, after all, and often handled large sums.

"Just call the bank, if you want. They'll tell you that amount will clear. If you will, call soon, so that if I decide on a vehicle today, I can write them a check, and they can verify it with you."

"I'll take care of it immediately. Here, let me give you a pad of checks." He reached in his desk drawer. "Do you want all this in checking, or do you want some of it in a savings account?"

"Put it all in checking for right now. I'll transfer some to savings later."

Dorie left the office and was headed for the front porch where Annie was sweeping, when she heard her housekeeper say something in the Cherokee language just as a vehicle drove up. Pushing the screen door open, Dorie saw a long automobile at the foot of the steps.

Jonah opened the driver's door and stepped out as Sarah bounced from the other side. "Look, Miss Dorie! Look, Annie! Uncle Jonah bought us a car!" She bounded up the steps. "Isn't it pretty?" She took Dorie by the hand and pulled. "Come see it!"

Dorie walked slowly toward the vehicle. Jonah stood, one hand on the roof, a big grin stretched over his face. "I hope you like it," he said.

"Why? It's your car." She knew it sounded hateful the minute the words were out of her mouth, but something in her just pushed them out. She couldn't get a handle on the whole situation, and it was making her cranky.

I owe him a car. Or a truck. Or something. I owe him. He saved me when I needed saving, and now he's gone and bought his own car. He doesn't need me for anything. He's going to leave. I know he is, but when I tried to get it over with, he wouldn't go. I don't know what's going to happen. Everything is totally out of control.

Jonah's smile faded, just a little, then he saw the humor in her bad-tempered answer. "It's a Lincoln," he said, as if that mattered. "A convertible. The top will go up or down, depending on the weather."

"Isn't it pretty?" Sarah asked. "See the dog on the front? It's a . . . a . . . what?" She turned to Jonah.

"A hood ornament—a greyhound."

"A greyhound." She looked up at Dorie to be sure she was listening. "That's a dog that goes really fast. This car can go really fast, too. Can't it, Uncle Jonah?"

"Well, I haven't tried it out going really fast yet, but the salesman said it would."

"Thought you were going to buy a truck, or maybe a car somewhat like mine."

"There are several trucks around the place, if we need one."

"I wanted a car like yours, Miss Dorie, but Uncle Jonah said we needed one that the whole family could ride in."

Eyebrows raised, she asked, "Whole family?"

"Your car only seats two. Even if I bought a sporty vehicle with a bench seat, it would only have room for three, growing more crowded as Sarah gets bigger. And when our family grows . . ."

"Grows?" Dorie was dazed with the idea.

"Yes," Sarah explained, "when I get a sister or brother, we'll need more room to ride."

"Sister or brother." Dorie was overcome with emotions, her eyes becoming glazed over as she tried to imagine such a thing.

"This car has a big backseat." Sarah opened one of the back doors in demonstration. "There'll be room for a bunch of us kids back here." She got in and moved along the leather seat to demonstrate.

"That's her idea, not mine," Jonah said. "I'd be happy with only a couple more."

Dorie was speechless. She wrapped her arms around herself and held on tight, else she might fall completely apart. Jonah turned her toward him and enveloped her in his arms.

"Don't worry. We'll take it slow, and we won't have any more children than you say we will." He pulled his arms back and sat her away so he could see her face. "You do want more children, don't you? More than just Sarah, I mean."

"I . . . uh . . ."

"We went to see a man while we were in town," Sarah informed her. "He was a . . . a what, Uncle Jonah?"

"A lawyer."

"Uncle Jonah went to see about making me his little girl, and the lawyer said, 'Doesn't your wife want to adopt her along with you?' and Uncle Jonah said, 'I haven't asked her yet.' You do, don't you, Miss Dorie? You do want to make me your little girl, don't you?" Her eyes were pleading.

Dorie looked deep into Jonah's eyes and then looked back at Sarah. "Of course I do. I certainly do want to make you my little girl." She would have said more, told Sarah how much she loved her, but Jonah kissed her right then, and it was some time before she could speak again.

Five weeks later, on the anniversary of their first, hurried ceremony, there was a wedding at the Big House. There were flowers and a wedding cake, and Reverend Lattimore was called on to repeat the words that were used the first time around, but this time the phrase "forever and ever" was included, at Sarah's insistence.

Dorie wore a simple, white silk dress and carried a bouquet of white roses with one pink bud in the center. Only she knew that it represented Dawn, whose mere existence brought this family together in the first place. Sarah preened in her own pink ensemble, which brought out the red hue in her hair. Annie was persuaded to wear a Cherokee tear dress, an outfit that in these modern times was usually delegated to special tribal ceremonies. Jonah said, "If this isn't a special ceremony, I don't know what is."

Jonah's parents and his brother, Thomas, were there from Waco, alleviating his mother's sadness over missing the original wedding. The brothers thought it was a very good thing that she had not been aware of what went on during the last year. Their parents were overjoyed at having Sarah close again, where they knew she was well cared for and they could see her often.

This family started forming a year ago, in tragedy, but at last it was official, and it would last forever and ever.

Epilogue

Sarah did eventually fly in an airplane, first as a passenger in her Uncle Thomas's plane, then later as a pilot. By the end of World War II, she was doing valuable war work, since almost all male pilots were occupied in America and overseas, working with the troops.

Thomas was unlucky in love for a long while. Later, he told his bride that he was waiting for the right woman to come along and she was late for their date.

Author's Comments

Although the town of Cottonport and surrounding area is fictional, many of the places mentioned in this book are actual localities. The area once called The Big Thicket was a wild and untamed area covering several counties in southeast Texas, home to both wild men and wild animals. It has been tamed over the decades and now looks like any other Texas landscape.

Galveston, Texas, played an important part in this book, but the Galveston of the past, not the present. Once called Sin City, it is now a delightful family vacation spot, with miles of beaches and interests and activities for folks young and old. Several places mentioned in *The Marriage Bargain* existed at one time, and some still do exist, although they have been "moved" a bit, chronologically, to make them fit into this fictional tale. The Galvez Hotel is still there, the premier hotel on Galveston Island. The Tremont Hotel existed in one location and exists now at another, but was not in operation in 1932. It is a super place to stay. I can vouch for it. Be sure to have a glass of wine on the roof while you're there. The Balinese Room existed in several incarnations, but not in 1932.

Galveston, Texas, was almost wiped off the face of the earth on September 8, 1900. With estimated winds of 145 miles per hour, the hurricane that struck killed between 8,000 and 12,000 people, compared to the 1,800 who died in Katrina. It is still the deadliest natural disaster to ever strike the United States.

The Brazos River flows into the Gulf of Mexico at Freeport, approximately 50 miles south of Galveston.

Also from **Soul Mate Publishing** and
Nancy Smith Gibson:

BETRAYAL ON THE BRAZOS

When Maggie Lancaster's uncle sent her to Texas to care for Cousin Annabelle's children, Maggie didn't expect Annabelle's husband to be disdainful or her cousin's murderer to show up at their ranch.

Jeb Sutton assumed his wife's cousin to be as useless and complaining as Annabelle had been, but he was surprised when Maggie adjusted to her new surroundings with ease. His children adored her and she loved them, too. Soon his attitude toward Maggie began to change.

When Maggie's former suitor shows up, it's time for Jeb to make his feelings clear and ask Maggie to stay forever.

Available now on Amazon: http://tinyurl.com/zpaz9s9

THE MEMORY OF ALL THAT

They tell her she's a cheating wife—a neglectful mother. She can't remember any of it. Her husband wants her memory to come back so she can tell them where her lover went with the plans and prototype for a secret government project. But if her memory returns, will she go back to being the selfish, narcissistic person she was in the past? She'd just as soon the past stays forgotten.

Available now on Amazon: http://tinyurl.com/jurzueb

GUSSIE AND THE CHEROKEE KID

When twenty-one-year-old Persephone Augusta Gomance is appointed to accompany a six-year-old orphan to her uncle in Texas, she is expecting to meet a wealthy ranch owner who is married to a schoolteacher and living in a fine home. When Travis Thacker, unmarried cardsharp, receives word that he is gaining custody of his niece Julia, he is expecting her chaperone to be an old battle-axe who will challenge his lifestyle. They are both in for a surprise. When Persephone and Travis first meet, sparks fly! The real trouble begins when Persephone receives a telegram with some unexpected news.

Full of comedy and sweet romance, this turn-of-the-century tale will have you laughing and rooting for the couple to work out their differences.

Available now on Amazon: http://tinyurl.com/j7vlzxl

CPSIA information can be obtained
at www.ICGtesting.com
Printed in the USA
FFOW01n1938140517
35532FF